1

This book is dedicated to;

Our boys, our imagination will take us to worlds that have not been discovered yet. Let's go on an adventure.

Prologue

Legend says that our star signs date from our ancient ancestors and the constellations in the skies. Only a few actually know the true tales behind them and how we have come to live by the zodiac signs. This story is largely about telling the true tales and legends of the zodiacs. There are many things still correct to this day such as the symbols and the character traits. But, so much is missing from these tales. Throughout the pages of this book you may discover much of the history and learn about the zodiacs that began to re-write the future. So much has changed too and that my dear, is where I come in. The name is Fynn and I am an Aquarian. Not like your modern day Aquarian or Aquarius as you humans call it now but one of the originals. I came to Earth many years ago with a group of my closest friends and allies.

We tend to keep ourselves to ourselves nowadays. We like the peace and tranquillity of the rainforest. You hear of those protected tribes, well that's us. We like to stay away from prying eyes. Oh, how times have changed. We would probably be captured and experimented on by the people of this planet nowadays.

I will start by telling you about the Libran's. They are a very spiritual and shy tribe. An ancient group of beings that love the peace and quiet. They prefer to live in areas of dense forestry, secluded and perfect for their way of life. They do not care for modern machinery or modern technologies and prefer only to use their own methods. In ancient days they were, as a rule, an elusive tribe. They avoided contact where possible with any outsiders.

They have excellent hearing abilities and this is largely due to them having a great curvature on their ears unlike other beings and they give excellent attention to detail in all aspects of their lives, especially taking great care when building their homes. Most Librans are tall creatures, almost elf like in appearance with ice coloured hair but there are a few exceptions. Royalty can be distinguished by looks as well as character. In ancient days they were tall creatures but today they generally match the likeness of humans in height. They possess the art of botany, mixing potions for rituals, magic and healing the wounded. They have a closeness like no other to the planet that they reside on and now to our beloved Mother Earth.

In recording their history the Librans were always somewhat relaxed, others would say lazy. Not all could read or write the articles needed to preserve history. They only cared to read and write fables, spell books and rituals for their potions and magic. There are some rare documents kept in secret and well hidden places around the world written by those that paved the way to the future. I myself am among the few who kept journals, scrolls and air looms in order to show the future generations the true accounts of the zodiacs.

Libran's like each of the zodiacs have their own peculiar words and customs. From the scarce tales and legends that have been documented it is likely that one would need an interpreter or translation device well versed in the ancient Libran language. In the earliest records kept, the librans had no royalty as such. They were a diplomatic tribe only led by their elders' wisdom and their faith. This changed over time once the elders had made a few mistakes and misconstrued guidance given by their beloved deity Hera that they worshipped

4

so devoutly. A quiet uprising began, or a change in tide as it were. When one Libran in particular began to question their judgement and rebel in a way that led to a new age beginning.

Hold up....wait a minute! I should probably start from the beginning of the story. The beginning of time. Well, not quite the beginning of time exactly but we'll just go with it.

It all started during the age of the gods, Zeus and one of his many wives Hera (who was also his sister might i add), ruled the universe and decided to send eleven of their children up to the skies to name a planet in the zodiac constellations, and build their own worlds using those planets. They had originally come from the constellations but they didn't actually create them as you humans believe. Each zodiac constellation has a planet named after the god or goddess that named it. In the Libra constellation, we have Hera named after the goddess Hera, who also went to the skies to name a planet; she birthed the Libran's and made them in her image.

In my constellation Aquarius, my home planet is named after my god Prometheus, we the Aquarian's are from a water world. Yes we dwell on land mostly but we are gifted with a magic that is sourced and found in water. Aquarian's are strong in stature and personality but wise enough to know when to bow down. We are like the Libran's and have no need for modern technologies or machinery and prefer to be independent.

We are speedy and stealthy which generally goes in our favour during wartime and times of trouble. In ancient times, we lived and prospered on our planet Prometheus but those days are long gone and we have since evolved as a species and moved on to find new homes. There are some preserved records kept on the Aquarian history throughout the ages but it is unlikely that any other race will understand our language.

The Cancerian planet Artemis, in their constellation was named by the goddess Artemis. The Cancerian's, well, what can I say? They are a magnificent species. Half-giant and extraordinarily strong. Most enemies will perish against these mighty beasts. They aren't the smartest of creatures but they are very loyal to their kin and to their allies. They have thickened and shell like skin, their own built in armour that is tough and durable. Not many blades can pierce through their own built-in defence mechanism but they do sometimes unfortunately have weaknesses and soft spots like all other species. In terms of their history, there were not many records kept or preserved. Only those on the history of the Cancerian's and their home planet Artemis that I have written and collected or those that my dearest friends kept in their journals. A dear friend would tell me fables and stories of her home and I made it my goal to preserve those historical moments for all of the Cancerian's of the future. The Cancerian's are blacksmiths by trade and hunters by nature, they are also great architects and builders despite their lack of wisdom. They do not like to settle or stay in one place too long unless it is absolutely necessary. Most would tell tales of how these creatures would eat anything that they laid eyes on but I'm not so sure on this now. In my lifetime, the Cancerian's that I have come to know and love are very picky about what they consume.

The Scorpio planet Kali, in their constellation was named by the goddess Kali. Every time that I think of the Scorpios their words ring through my ears.

In a kingdom full of storms,

we arise and strike the sword,

Deep into the darkness we go,

Our survival Is the future.

They were right... deep into the darkness we went. Until we found the light.

The Scorpio's were warriors and survivors. But first and foremost they were a race of wondrous wizards. They possessed power like no other and a passion for magical objects. Lots of historical evidence can be found on their magic and lore in spell books today. The spells have been adapted and modified throughout the ages. As for evidence of historical events and their home planet Kali, these scrolls and air looms are kept in the Kali historical library. The location is kept a secret, so secret in fact that it is magically warded and invisible. Only a few know where it is and how to get in. The Scorpio's as a race are known to be brave, ambitious and loyal. They certainly lived up to those traits in my experience.

When some Scorpios have been too ambitious and impatient in the past it has been known to get them into some tricky situations. The Scorpios have also got their own language, very different to anything seen before. When writing the scorpion letters they appear as hieroglyphs or runes on the pages. Experts have been known to find and decipher the occasional mysterious article. Luckily, none so far have been curses or dark magics that would render the unwitting and unfortunate soul deformed or worse. Dead.

The Taurean planet Aphrodite, that is in the Taurus constellation and was named by the goddess Aphrodite. She was a warrior goddess and birthed the Taureans. She was also the goddess of love and the Taureans were and are fierce and vicious warriors when it comes to going against those who have harmed their kin. They were built like strong bulls but were the most loving and affectionate species of all, in fact procreation was a monthly festivity back in the old days. They are wise but let their hearts lead them. Sometimes into devastation. Much can be learned from their history and from my dear friend Tor. He is the timekeeper for our world, he is the ultimate zodiac historian. He has been a mentor to myself and my dear friends for most of our existence. He taught us the Taurean language and the ways of the old worlds. I will forever be thankful.

The Gemini planets Athena One and Athena Two were named by the goddess Athena and these are the home planets to the Gemini race. They are blessed with a coupling magic, they are nimble warriors that can divide into two and this gift allows them to overpower the enemy. They are small and fast, can weave quickly through hoards and defeat them from behind enemy lines. The warriors work in unison with their doppelganger and it will mirror each move that they make. They are known as the tricksters of the zodiacs. They love to joke and play games on us, it does give us some entertainment in the forest now when times get a little mundane. The Gemini can communicate with its twin internally and give instructions on what it should do, it can be heard by others but this language has never been deciphered by any other creature alive or any zodiac. But, we do have a common tongue developed and spoken by all zodiacs now so that we can communicate with them. We have since catalogued and recorded the history of the Gemini and their home planets to share with future generations.

The planet Apollo in the Leo constellation was named after the god Apollo and is home to the Leo's. A fierce league of glorious and regal beings. Led by the King of the Leo's, they are a force to be reckoned with. King Corin and I have painstakingly crafted all of the historical scrolls over the last few centuries that had been lost forever. The history is now set in stone and in scroll. The Leo's as a people are very passionate and generous. The great King Corin has a quiet confidence about him but there have been times where he appears to be very arrogant. But would you expect any less from a King? Over the years we have brought history to life. He would tell myself and our group of scribes great and glorious stories of mighty victories in battle and devastating defeats alike.

The planet Demeter is home to the Virgo and is in the Virgo constellation and this was named by the goddess Demeter. The Virginians have the gift of sight. Foresight to be exact and can project their visions from their third eye to show fellow zodiacs the future, as well as the past and the present. Even the young are extremely wise, it is their nature. The Virgo as a people are kind, patient and very hardworking. They, two in particular, along with the Capricorn have taken on the role of adviser's and counsel to our leaders and this balance works well for the most part.

The planet Zeus in the Sagittarius constellation was named by Zeus himself and is home to the Sagittarian's. He crafted these skilful archers and made them perfect in every way, they are and always have been a zodiac race to worship. They are the ultimate foot soldier and protectors of the realm. When they are in combat they are quick to rain terror through the skies down onto the enemy. Historical symbols and magical relics can be found in places located on all of the planets in the zodiac constellations and these will open up and bless the knowledge and history for those that are worthy to become enlightened.

The Capricorn planet was named after the goddess Persephone. The Capricorn took on the role as advisers and counsel to our royalty. They are practical, realistic and so very disciplined. You will find their historical articles to be very well organised in the Capri Library and historical society. I, myself find the rituals and discipline a little too restrictive at times but we have worked well together in the past.

The Pisces planet was named after the goddess Ishtar. Oh dear Pearl, how I miss my Piscean friend at times. She is deep in the ocean somewhere playing a long game of hide and seek. They will rise up from the depths of the ocean one day and reveal themselves to you humans. There have been legends of sirens singing in the seas but no, that is the Piscean singing their beautiful song.

The planet in the Aries constellation was named after the god of war Ares. They are passionate, motivated and confident leaders. They have a relentless determination and with this we made it to mother earth unscathed. They are built like rams with a golden fleece and do sometimes clash with one another due to them being such passionate creatures. There have been many times that I have had to dissolve disputes between King Corin of the Leo's and Lord Shofar of the Aries clan. Most historical articles that involve the Aries nation are detailing battles and war. They thrive on it.

There is one constellation missing from this, the Ophiuchus constellation, the serpent bearer that was named after Laocoon, Poseidon's Trojan priest. Why? You ask...well I guess you will have to continue the story to find out. These were not the only planets in the zodiac constellations either. Many gods joined them and forty-eight were brought into existence. But we will just focus on the ones that I have mentioned already.

Anyway, back to the truth. It was twelve thousand years ago to this very day. Yes, we have lived long and we are old, so very old. We came from Hera, the Libran planet which orbited the star Beta Librae. When we found Earth after what had felt like a millennium of space flight, 160 years at light speed to be exact. We were so very relieved to feel the sand, soil, and stones underneath our feet.

Kora, well she was ecstatic. Earth reminded my Libran friend so much of home. The home she so deeply grieved for. Our lifespans back home were not quite as long as here on Earth. I'm not sure why? Maybe the fact that the blasted serpents cut them short.

I often think back to those times and wonder what would happen had we stayed? After years and years of adventure, war, loss, laughter, and love.

CHAPTER ONE

She stood on the bank of the Lagoon with water dripping down her bare arms. Glancing down as she felt it trickle, thinking that a bug had landed on her. She shook her arm and laid her hand where the drip had tickled her. It's late afternoon, the day star is still beaming high in the sky. Beating down onto the forest, through gaps in the dense foliage like bright white laser strips. The trees standing over two hundred feet tall with thick and fragrant wisteria drooping all the way down, reflecting light rays in all directions. A rainbow of blue, orange and purple flows throughout the forest during the long and warm hours of daylight. The forest floor littered with wild-flowers and plants, glowing and whistling along to the sounds of the wildlife.

The smallest of plants scattered beside the pathways, clattering and tapping along as if they are mimicking the sounds of the forest dwellers that are building and working away in the trees.

See, the forest is alive and the forest dwellers are very respectful of that. They wait and listen for signs that the tree has passed and that its essence has left its carcass before building new homes into the trees. It almost sounds like sweet and harmonic music if one listens closely enough.

"Kora!... Where are you, Kora!?" A distant voice yells from the village outskirt.

"Oh no! Not now!" she groaned while she imagined the stern and disapproving look on Ailah's face.

"Kora!?"

"Ugh! Yes!...OK, Aunt Ailah! I'm coming!" the young beauty bellows as she drags herself from the water again, skin glowing, whilst ringing the water from her locks. Sweeping her curling mane backward and covering herself in her clothes and leathers.

'I wonder what Aunt Ailah wants.' She grumbles under her breath a little.

Walking through the woodland to make her way home, she is constantly in awe of how much beauty envelops her. Kora and her kin live inside the trees, at one with nature. Ailah is standing by the stairs at the bottom of her house, that is one hundred feet above, waiting patiently but with a stern and troubled look in her eye. Kora gazes at her straight silver-white hair not moving one bit as if frozen by ice, her pale white skin that looks as if it hasn't aged in half a century and her shocking green eyes that seem to glow brighter when she sometimes laughs.

'What did you need Ailah?'

'Kora, a messenger of the elders came earlier, you have been chosen, you must prepare for the pairing ceremony.' she says with a rather numb tone.

There is a hint of sadness there. She has always been hard on Kora because of her wild ways and unruly behavior or at least that's what she has always said. Apparently, she has been quite the rebel at times. She respects her aunt though; she had given up her own chance of being paired and raising a family to take care of her niece. She felt that it was her duty to take Kora as her own when her parents passed.

Within the tribe, some say that she is one shining star, a young lass whose beauty is indescribable, her long locks of hair, curling and waving, thrashing about like a windy ocean. She not only stands out from the rest because of her mesmerizing beauty. She is always playful and speaks her mind.

A free spirit, despite what the other forest dwellers say, the elders do not like it. She loves to sing, dance and play boisterous games. They fear that one day this little Libran may bring tragedy to the tribe. Always play fighting and sparring when she knows that it will be frowned upon. What they don't know, is that she has been training secretly for years after copying the boys with their fighting techniques.

"She should know her place!" The elders would yell at Ailah.

"She is not to fight! The boys will have their duties and she will have hers!"

Some of the tribe cannot understand why she looks different to them. She has blood red hair, and they all have icy white hair. She is different, and it makes them nervous.

"We must return home to prepare Kora, the pairing is tomorrow and we need to have you fitted and I must make your ceremonial dress, and tonight there will be a feast for the whole tribe to attend."

'The feasts are always such glorious events with food, nectar, singing, dancing, games, and stories. Come to think of it, it was around this time last year that there was a feast for the whole tribe, odd. Deep down, it doesn't feel like a celebration, something is wrong I can feel it'. Kora thinks whilst filling with dread and realization that soon she will have to leave home.

"Oh Aunt Ailah, I don't want this?! Why did they choose me?!"

"Kora! It is not the elders who choose, it is the Goddess Hera who chooses and gives guidance to the elders, Do you question the goddess?!"

"No, I do not question the goddess, I just do not want to leave."

"It is your duty, that is enough now, you will do as you are told for once! We must prepare, hurry!" Ailah said as she hurried Kora up the stairs that twisted and turned around the gigantic tree trunks. Vines and roots snaking off in all directions with bridges that linked them together.

There are hundreds of homes in the trees. All with big round doorways carved into them, ornate with vines and oakwood figures set into the borders. Aunt Ailah's doorway has brilliant orange flower petals hanging down rather than a door like other forest dwellers. It doesn't really matter too much, about having a door because it is warm all year round and it is safe. Kora has gotten used to going to sleep listening to the sound of raindrops loudly crashing against the leaves and branches as they fall. She had grown to love that sound as she was growing up, along with the squeaking and turning of the pulley systems as tools, food, and supplies were being lifted from the ground.

They are finally home. It always feels like a tiring and treacherous climb, ascending one hundred feet up the stairways and bridges. Kora is grateful that they don't live closer to the sky like many of the others.

"I wonder what games there will be tonight Aunt Ailah, I always love the festive games."

"Oh, I am sure there will be many, but I am afraid you will not be joining the games tonight Kora, you will be blessed and painted for the pairing. Now, come, let us fit you for your dress before the day disappears."

After hours of being poked and prodded, the pairing gown is ready and it is almost time for the feast to begin. Aunt Ailah informs her she is one of fifteen to be chosen.

"Let us make our way to the feast, young one, come along now." Aunt Ailah orders as she leaves and begins the descent to the forest floor.

Following slowly and hesitantly, gazing through the trees and foliage at all the critters and creatures floating about. The multicolored flowers dotted throughout the forest. Kora takes a deep breath and inhales the sweet fragrant smell of the blooming plants.

"I guess I have to leave home then" she sighs. "It's what Hera wants."

Most of the forest dwellers have already arrived. Kora follows her aunt and sits by the fire that is crackling and spitting out small pieces of ash that float off into the sky before disappearing altogether.

"Eat now Kora, you will be painted soon."

She does as she is told reluctantly and quickly eats some soup that has been passed to her by a young Libran and then makes her way towards the elders. They are preparing the burning sage and petals while mixing the silver shell paint. Kora notices that the colour of the paint resembles the blade of her bone dagger that she has hidden in a nearby hollowed tree stump. They were an odd pair of fellows, all wrinkly, bald and old, muttering away whilst preparing for the ritual. Flicking petals and nectar about chanting to Goddess Hera with their pointed ears twitching a little as they moved about. Kora waited patiently in line, on her knees, like the other girls, to be decorated like a prize about to be given away. She was to be offered up as a bride.

The elders continued to chant and hum whilst decorating the young girl's arms with a beautiful tribal pattern that swirled up and down and side to side. The paint had an aroma that was metallic but mixed with the damp algae that floated at the edges of the lagoon that Kora would often visit. They added different symbols, runes and marks on their chests and foreheads too that appeared as if it were jewelry. Waving the sage and blessing them, the ritual was complete.

The girls walked the path around the floor of the forest village, passing the other chanting and humming villagers who would place glowing, pearlescent white flower chains over their necks and around their arms. Until they all reached the fire again where they were given their first ever drink of the nectar from the Ancient temple tree. This always made them woozy and relaxed so that they would sleep better. This was like an initiation into womanhood. They were no longer girls anymore, the goddess has blessed them, they are ready.

Soon the dark of night crept in and it was time to climb and head to bed. For the following morning, the elders would take the young brides to meet their betrothed and to complete the pairing ceremony. After the pairing ceremony is complete, they will have only a short time before they have to leave home to become wives, or so they thought. Kora fell to sleep with such ease that night.

CHAPTER TWO

It felt like morning had approached too quickly as Kora awoke to Ailah telling her to rise from her slumber and get up out of bed.

"It is morning young one, you must prepare yourself and be dressed for the ceremony."

"OK, I'm getting up now." sighed Kora whilst rubbing her weary eyes, not wanting to move from her fur-covered bed. Feeling as if she had grown roots and become planted overnight. Her head is still woozy from the nectar.

She sat up and glanced at the beautiful dress placed at the foot of her bed, then looked at the paint still covering her body. It is still perfectly in place and hasn't smeared one bit. She slipped the dress on and brushed through her hair with a wooden comb. It had been carved from a piece of the root buttress tree that had passed. The dress was covered in silver Libran decor embroidered down the middle right to knees with symbols that looked like scales.

"Here, you must put on this veil as well Kora, and do not remove it until you are given a signal." Ailah passed a white silk veil that would cover the lower part of the face and only show Kora's beautiful and dazzling blue eyes. It was fixed with a shining silver rope that tied at the back. It's time to start the journey to the temple and meet her betrothed.

The walk is almost silent, all the way, the whole three kilometres north, through the dense forest pathway, it will take almost half a day.

Upon approaching the temple Kora can feel herself getting more and more anxious.

Once inside, the elders position the girls into a half moon shape. The betrothed are already there waiting, standing in silence until the elders have placed them all, chanting, blessing each one of them as they went. Kora nervously looked directly across at the other beings. Huge and ugly from what she could make out. They are not a Libran tribe.

She couldn't really see much though as they also had their faces covered with black and gold veils. They are dressed in black and gold as if it were to match the likeness of what the Libran's are wearing. Only the symbols look different. A being holding a serpent rather than scales.

Maybe it means that they are more worthy than us if they are wearing black with gold. She pondered.

"It could be why we must think of being chosen as a privilege?"

With the elders still chanting, the males begin to step forward one by one. But, each time they do the girl opposite steps forward when the elder steps behind her and taps her on the shoulders with both hands until she is directly before his feet. It is Kora's turn to step forward. Whilst every ounce of her

21

is screaming to turn and run, she forces her small feet one by one to move. Crunching through the dead leaves that spread through the room until she has assumed the position. Keeping her eyes fixed firmly to the ground through fear of looking up and crying out.

Eventually, she gathers the courage to look up slowly at this beast until she makes direct eye contact with him. Filling with even more horror and dread, a wrenching feeling in the pit of her stomach, resisting the urge to wretch when she realises how unpleasant her betrothed really is even before removing his veil.

He looks as if he is half-libran and half serpent. Snake-like, with beady black eyes and green scales across half of his face. She continues to search for recognisable features on his face but she just can not see any. The only resemblance that she can find is his body. Although, he is much larger and stronger looking. He gives off an aroma of dead rotting animals. Ghastly.

The chanting gets louder and louder, petals being thrown at their feet, each pair, one by one removing the veils to reveal themselves to the betrothed...then silence.

It feels like the silence has lasted a lifetime. She can feel this horrid creature's eyes glaring at her, sizing her up as if she were a meal.

"Why? Why would they do this?" she thought.

Suddenly, a rush of vivid and blinding images comes flooding in. A flashback, she remembers a chosen bride many years ago. She recalls seeing her being dragged away, kicking and screaming by what must have been the collection point in the forest and by whom must have been her betrothed.

"Why was she screaming out like that? I have to find out what happened. Surely she would have been honoured to have been chosen to carry out this tradition?"

Snapping back to the real world and taking another nervous gaze at this beast standing tall before her.

His beady black eyes piercing through her. She glances at him, up and down, to see his huge biceps all grey and scaly. Covered in black ink with a ritualistic pattern. He looks as if he has been tortured or harmed during a battle, with scars and stripes dotted all over his face and chest. Kora can hear a rumbling coming from his chest when he takes a breath, despite not saying a word she knows that his voice will be deep and deafening.

"Why would they pair us with these awful creatures?"

The Elders signal that the ceremony is now complete. Kora is glad that it is over. Following the elders, the girls walk out in a single file orderly manner, despite wanting to run.

Kora is filled with so many questions and can feel the anger building as if it's a volcano about to erupt. No wonder the girl acted so strangely. It feels like someone has just signed her death sentence.

"Why do we have such a strange tradition? Why not pair us with other forest-dwelling Libran tribes? They didn't even exchange names with us, they didn't speak."

Watching as the girls walked out of the temple Kora's betrothed Seth who is the Ophiuchus Prince Daimon's right hand, glanced from side to side at his brothers in arms.

"Those females look weak and feeble" he remarked in a frustrated manner with his deep and husky voice.

"Come, now that is over, let us go and feast before returning to the city!" he yelled as he left the temple and mounted his salamander. The march back to the city had begun.

'Stupid girls' he thought.

'How can they blindly follow and do as they are told without question. They will learn...what their purpose truly is. Vile little creatures. That one with the red hair looked so familiar. Why is she different from the rest? Did I draw the short straw and get the runt?'

CHAPTER THREE

Deep in the forest in a deserted homestead, just outside another Libran settlement, in the swooping and fertile lands, an elderly Libran sat huddled with a few of his companion escapees. Crouched in the corner of the wooden shack that had been left unfinished, behind stacks of redwood planks.

One of his companions had been badly wounded. Flesh torn and flapping from his jaw, around the bare and splintered bone that pierced through his face.

His eye swollen like a balloon to the point where it looked as if it would pop. Blood congealed around the gashes, cuts and the gaping hole. He had fallen and injured himself running from the Ophiuchus. His friends had refused to leave him and press on with their escape when the Ophiuchus were bound to slither up at any moment. A group of serpent soldiers along with their commander had been hot on their tails since they had escaped two days prior.

He had slowed them down and lost them the advantage of speed and haste. The night was fast approaching and now they were trapped.

They could hear the serpents heckling and taunting them as they surrounded the shack. Circling and hissing at them as they dismounted their salamander beasts.

He knew that this was the end. There would be no mercy from the serpents. The pure evil that ran through their veins, they had been created by the Trojan Priest himself. They were driven by hatred, malice and ignorance.

The Libran had heard whispers of the queen coming to liberate him one day and had decided to try and escape. In order to guide the chosen one toward his kin and the settlement. For her to free them from the serpent's grasp.

There were stories of increasing violence and torture circulating the settlement. Reports of Librans being burned alive, whipped and cut to pieces just for fun and amusement.

All of the women and children had been taken and imprisoned somewhere and put to the sword or axe, with their bleeding corpses strung from the pyres, carrion for the beasts.

The wounded companion was losing consciousness. Whimpering and groaning softly as he faded into the light. The colour of death sweeping over him like a sheet. The friends all rested their hands on him and bowed their heads in prayer.

The Ophiuchus are hacking the door down now, laughing and jeering as they smashed through. It would not be long before they were found now.

One of the youngest companions, a boy, no older than ten years began to cry. Tears streaming silently and hopelessly down his cheeks.

The door fractured into a hundred pieces, splinters flying off in all directions as the serpents burst through. Eyes wide and piercing.

There were six of them inside the shack and probably many more outside. The commander, Seth slithered in with the soldiers silently. A cold killer waiting to catch his prey. Expressionless, he stepped towards the elderly Libran and without saying a word picked him up effortlessly. His feet dangling in the air, throat constricted by the clenching fist around it.

He gave orders for the others to be dragged away and slaughtered.

He lifted his scaly arm and thrust his blade into his victims stomach. Twisting it as he pulled out again. For a moment he stared into his eyes watching his life slip away from his body with pure satisfaction. He raised his arm up again and plunged his sword into the man's skull, then proceeded by flinging him from his blade like a rag doll.

The others tried to fight off the serpents and run but they could not outrun the salamander beasts. Within moments all of them lay dead, strewn about the floor in pieces. All but one were slain.

The young boy stood frozen, eyes filled with fear and terror. Feet soaking in his friends' blood that had flooded the grounds.

The commander thought it would be amusing to let this one go. 'Try and run to your queen he taunted'.

'Tell her that we are ready and waiting for the slaughter' he continued.

The boy ran for his life, as far and as fast as he could until the serpents chased him no more.

CHAPTER FOUR

Back in the village after the long journey home. Kora wastes no time in making the climb and visiting Nanuu to seek the answers that she so desperately needs, quickly stopping to collect her bone dagger from a hollowed out tree and slipping it down the back of her belt. Nanuu always knows what to do despite being a tad scatty and crazy.

She is another villager, who has been like a grandmother to Kora. She is almost as old and wrinkly as the elders. But, she is certainly not as mean and grumpy. A little dumpy old woman and she tells amazing tales. Kora always loved to hear her tales growing up, they always seemed to be so real. There was a tale about a king and a queen fighting for their people but losing the fight after many years of battle. *What funny stories they were, this tribe has never been in a battle and they have always lived in peace in the forest. Kora thought to herself.*

"Come in my dear, I have been expecting you, I knew that you would visit as soon as you had returned."

Nanuu croaked whilst swinging on her makeshift indoor hammock, almost spinning upside down. She always did like to have fun. Nanuu hopped off of her hammock like a little hopping toad and walked toward the dusty doorway, surrounded by pots and flowers, wiggling her wide bottom from side to side.

Kora tiptoed in through the doorway barefoot. The smooth wooden boards that had been waxed with tree sap under her toes, is strangely satisfying. They had been worn over the years of Nanuu living there but treated very well. She takes a moment to observe the room and to take in the feeling of nostalgia. She would play there a lot as a child. The curved shelves around the walls that held all of Nanuu's pots, pans, and treasures. She had laid out vibrant flowers on them to make it more colourful. All the blankets and shawls hanging everywhere reminded Kora of her den making days. They would drape them over the hammock and across the floor for comfort and then they would lay, talk, giggle and tell tales for hours.

"Come and sit down, it is time... I must tell you something," Nanuu said sincerely whilst holding Kora's hand pulling her towards a rug made from giant red titan arum leaves in front of the open fire.

She had grown plump and wrinkly in her old age, her hair frizzing, tucked behind her ears. She was not tall like the other Librans, she was short and dumpy. She would joke and say it made her more nimble and easier to hide when playing games with the little ones.

"Nanuu, I have so many questions." Kora sighed.

"Hush, Hush, Hush my dear"...

Nanuu gazed up, as she sat cross-legged like a praying elder, wrapped in a brown shawl weaved from feather plants, that covered most of her lumps and bumps. Wanting to waste no time Nanuu proceeded.

"You must visit the goddess Hera's temple dear young one, you will find your answers there. You must make an offering to the goddess of the blue poppy flower, a little of your blood, and some moonstone."

Here, I have some moonstone in my treasure chest. You must go to the poppy fields and pick the flower, It must be blue! Not black or red, but blue! Just a droplet of your blood will do."

"The temple is the final resting ground of our beloved goddess Hera. It is one kilometre East of the forest, you will find the blue poppy field next to it."

Nanuu passes the white stone to Kora as she gets up again and hurries her out of the door.

"Now... I am old, I must rest again, I have not been to sleep for a whole one hour," Nanuu states as she climbs back onto her hammock and begins to snore as if she is catching glow-flies.

Kora leaves feeling a little bemused, she never could get a word in with Nanuu.

She decided that she would go to the temple the following morning.

CHAPTER FIVE

Later that day, Kora is sitting by the lagoon dangling her feet in the water making little splashes and watching the glistening ripples radiate across the water. She hears rustling coming from the trees, a boy stumbling towards her. He's injured and whimpering. As he reaches her he falls to his knees and collapses on her lap.

She panics and carries him to the village shouting for help. The Librans come rushing to help and gather around Kora and the boy. Ailah pushes through them fearing that Kora had been hurt in some way.

"Who is this Kora?"

"I don't know Ailah, he just ran towards me and collapsed. He must be from another village".

Librans began whispering and muttering amongst themselves airing concerns. The boy begins to wake, he looks up at Kora and weakly says "They killed them all, they killed my family".

Ailah orders Kora to bring the boy to the Elders for his wounds to be treated. Kora looks up in agreement and nods to Ailah before scooping him up into her arms again. As she is carrying him, she whispers " its ok now boy, you are safe".

" My name is Felix and none of us are safe, they are coming".

"Who is coming?" Kora worries.

"Th.. Th.. The Ophiuchus" he says with a shake in his voice.

As Kora is walking through the village with Felix in her arms, she glances down at his pale and delicate face. The boy could barely be ten years old. Covered in cuts and bruises, the most significant bruises around his wrists from being restrained. His icy white hair muddied by blood that couldn't possibly be his own.

Kora reaches the Elders without saying a word or even looking at her, they quickly take the boy to care for his wounds and send her back home to Ailah.

As Kora reaches home, night is falling and the stars are lighting the sky. Ailah is sitting waiting for her. Kora asks as she sits down beside Ailah "who are the Ophiuchus?".
Ailah stares through the door at the starry sky momentarily before looking at Kora and stating softly "You are betrothed to an Ophiuchus Kora".
Kora jumps up and begins pacing up and down, ranting and raving at how disgusting they are." Why would you want me to pair with something like that? This is not what Hera wants".
Ailah pleads with Kora to turn a blind eye and do as she's told for the good of her own tribe. "We must look after our own Kora, we must keep them safe!".

Infuriated, Kora storms towards her bedroom and yells "I am going to bed, tomorrow I am going to get answers".

CHAPTER SIX

Rising early the next morning, before Ailah awoke. Kora gathers her bone dagger and some food for the walk in her satchel. It is still dark out. The plants light the forest at night. She makes a hasty descent sweeping her hand along the moist vines that appeared as if they held up the stairways. Tiptoeing down until she can feel the grit and soil beneath her toes. She begins her walk towards the temple through the forest and fields.

After walking all day and getting a little lost, Kora can finally see the temple and a blanket of blue poppies in a nearby field. She gathers the petals, takes her bone dagger and slices her hand. Searing pain shot through Kora's hand and up through her arm as the blade sliced across it and took her breath away. 'Mistake' she thought as she remembered Nanuu telling her that only a drop was needed. Every part of the wound oozed with blood and it pooled and spilled over the side like a scarlet waterfall. She tipped the blood onto the foot of the statue of Hera in front of her as tears welled in her eyes. Kora felt as if she would pass out from the pain.

Each droplet reminded her of her life. Each droplet reminded her of the lies. She stopped for a moment and remembered everything that had led up to this moment. Hopefully the beloved Hera would give her the truth and not lies and stories like she had been told throughout her entire life.

Crushing them together with the moonstone and begins pleading to Hera.

"Oh, Hera, dear ancient one, the giver of light, show me what I must see. Show me the journey ahead, what must I do? Show me what I must see"

She places the offering onto the stone altar and dips the tips of her finger into it. She smears the petals and blood onto the statue that she had knelt before and then proceeds by smearing it on her forehead in the shape of a Libran symbol.

Suddenly, a powerful gust of wind begins to swoop around her. Twisting, twirling and turning in circles. Kora can hear voices whispering and chanting as if it is being carried by the wind. It is growing louder and louder but she cannot understand what it means.

It lifts her off the ground in her kneeling position. Floating in the air. Kora's eyes roll into the back of her skull and then darkness. Kora had blacked out.

She opens her eyes moments later like a newborn opening its eyes for the very first time, it takes a few moments to adjust to the bright light, it almost hurts a little bit and she can see what is before her. She is standing in the centre of a battleground. All different creatures, including Libran's at war. Fighting the Ophiuchus. The Serpent grooms.

'What does this mean?'

Then, it's as if she is flying above it. Through the soldiers hacking and slashing, the brutal fighting, the blood, and gore.

Hearing the deafening screams of soldiers and the clangs of weapons hitting other weapons, the thundering, the marching, it was horrifying. Kora saw a familiar looking man standing in the centre of it all. Looking so very sad. He wore robes and armour around his body. She is unsure of why she feels like she knows him.

He is looking at the death and destruction before him feeling hopeless as his soldiers are being torn down and cut to pieces by the serpents. This was a King. A Libran King losing a battle to save his people. Kora notices that this King is holding a carved wooden staff with gems set into it, but it looks broken. A piece is missing from the top. A piece that resembles the handle of Kora's bone dagger.

'I must find this weapon.'

Kora felt herself plummeting. Like she was falling from the sky towards the sharp and deadly weapons.

Thud!

'Ouch!'

Kora opens her eyes, and she is back in the temple laid on the hard, cold ground. It's morning again. She had been there all night.

'My betrothed is my enemy. Why were they at war?'

Kora sits up, still feeling dizzy and confused.

"I need to find that staff. I still have so many unanswered questions. Even more so now."

Looking toward the statue again, Kora notices a crumpled piece of cloth. It is a map.

She recalls that as she opened her eyes, the goddess whispered to her.

"Go to Amoran city Kora, find the pendant."

CHAPTER SEVEN

Kora observed the map and realised that she had quite the journey ahead of her, she recalled seeing the Libran King. She grieved for him. Knowing that her kind were always so firm and strong. Yet they would always be diplomatic and try to please everyone.

"How did this war happen? Why?"

She set off on her three-day trek, not wanting to waste any more time. Barely giving a thought to Aunt Ailah who was probably searching the forest tirelessly for her niece.

'I must press on, I cannot go home, Ailah will keep me there, I will not be able to leave again'

"You must let her complete this Journey Ailah!" Nanuu demanded as she glared at Ailah stood between the Elders. "I sent her to seek advice from Hera in the temple and this is obviously the path that Hera has laid out for our Kora. Maybe she will bring justice to our people and not tragedy like you old fools believe" she scorned and frowned at the Elders.

"Nanuu she will die! She is but a young girl, a young and naive girl! They will find out that she is gone and then they will know that our treaty is broken and kill us all... just like the other settlements." Ailah cried out.

"Ah, she is a young girl you say? Yet not too young for you to send her off to be paired? Despite your sworn vows to her parents? Let us trust in Hera's wisdom and see how this unfolds"

As the treacherous hike was coming to a close, days and nights of climbing mountains and cliffs, crawling over hills and valleys. Sleeping under the moons and stars. How cold those nights were. Heading towards Amoran city. Kora had grown weary and sore. She stopped near a small wood to rest under the cover of the plants and giant leaves for a while.

'Never been this far from home. Oh, what I would do for my fur covers and some warm broth right now.' she thought to herself as she blew hot air into her cold hands to try and warm up.

"Whomp! Whomp! Whomp!"

Kora heard a loud thudding sound. It sounded like marching and drumming. She covered herself quickly in the undergrowth and hid behind a tree, moss staining her cheeks. Eyes darting around like an animal being hunted, searching for the direction in which its predator was coming for the kill.

Kora could not see where the noise was coming from until she looked up and realised that she was not actually in a woodland. She was in some trees that sat at the bottom of the city walls.

'The noise must be coming from above.'

Listening again. She could hear rushing water. Like a waterfall hitting the pool at the bottom.

'I wonder who is up there? I need a closer look.'

Looking around for somewhere to climb she spots some cracks in the enormous stone bricks that she could slip her toes into and grip them as if she were climbing a ladder. Crawling up the wall as quietly as possible, like a bug on a tree in the forest, she reached the top.

Peeping over as carefully as she could. She instantly spotted the serpent soldiers marching up and down beating drums.

"Hey! Get Down! They will see you and capture you!" a voice whispered with panic.

Kora ducked down for a moment and waited for the soldiers to pass again. She climbed over quickly and hid behind a stack of straw bales that had been propped nearby.

"Over here!" The voice yelled. "To your right!"

Turning around to see a tower on her right with a small and splintered wooden door cracked open. She could see someone waving her in.

"You're a Libran aren't you!? My name is Fynn. I'm an Aquarian. It's lovely to meet you and all. But, what are you doing here!? Trying to get yourself killed?"

"Err...Aquarian? Get myself killed? What do you mean? Who are you?"

"Yes, I am an Aquarian. Don't you know what we are? And those beady eyes out there will kill you if they see you here!" said Fynn.

"Kora... my name is Kora. I am from the Libran forest. I am here to find the pendant. The Goddess Hera sent me." Kora stated sheepishly as she glanced up at this blue-skinned being.

He looked almost like her but he was blue with silver eyes that sparkled like a newly buffed shield. His skin almost glittering when the light shines through the cracks in the door and hits it. It reminds Kora of the lagoon water that would glimmer when the light rays and beams would shoot down. The hair on his head resembled waves crashing against the shore. Mesmerising.

"That will be in the throne room. It's not used much anymore since the Libran King is gone and all."

"What happened here?"

"The war happened Kora, we Aquarians are kept as slave workers for the Ophiuchus. They shackled us and we have to source water for them. We don't have time for that. Let's Go! I'll show you where it is! Be careful, we must not get caught!"

Fynn grabbed Kora's hand and pulled her through the narrow corridors stopping now and then to listen and look out for trouble. His hand was ice cold and wet. He had a strange rusted metal band around his wrist that looked as if it didn't belong.

"What is this?" Kora whispered.

"It stops me from shifting. It's how they keep us enslaved here. You know? The shackle I mentioned."

"Shifting? What is Shifting?"

"You don't know anything, do you? I am an Aquarian. Water? I can shape-shift and control water. You are a Libran, Yes? You represent Justice. Therefore, you need the staff of Amoran to unlock your power but your kind also possesses the knowledge of botany?."

"The staff!? The goddess Hera showed me the staff! I must find it!"

Fynn chuckles. "Yes sweet girl, you must"

"Now, we must follow this corridor and slip to the right and up the stairs. Then hope and pray to your goddess that there isn't a slithering soldier in the throne room at the top."

As Kora and Fynn approach the door, they notice that the throne room is silent. The coast is clear to enter and begin their hunt. As they step in, Kora realises that they are standing behind a deep blue velvet curtain that is draped down from the roof. It has the Libran symbol, in silver embossed all over it. It is glorious.

She popped her head around the heavy curtain for a moment, the dust tickling her nose and she begins to sneeze. She peers around and gazes upon the decadent room. The throne that is sat at the centre of the stage is made from silver-white moonstone that is marbled and is engraved with the most beautiful decoration she has ever laid eyes on. Strange symbols and pictures all over it, as if they tell a story. It is dazzling, Kora can see her own face in the reflection. Fynn awkwardly catches her pulling faces at herself.

She paces around the throne scanning the walls, the shelves, the windows that stretch twenty feet up to the ceiling in this royal room, telling herself to be more serious. The painted glass shattered and cracked. Remnants and shards still scattered all over the floor. It has never been cleaned up.

"Over there!" Fynn exclaimed as he spotted a small walnut chest on one of the wall shelves.

Kora grabbed the box and opened it, but not before observing the beautiful Libran craftsmanship. She could smell the sweet scent of the wood. Smoothing her fingers across the lid to feel the grooves in the pattern and slowly opening the chest, she sets eyes on one single ruby jewel on a chain. Beautiful.

"It's the pendant, this is the pendant that the ancient one told me to find!"

"That is great but we must be going now! Before we are found! Come, we will go the way we came and climb down the wall that you climbed up, yes, I am coming with you, I cannot be a slave here any longer."

CHAPTER EIGHT

Back in the Libran forest Ailah is waking from her slumber, she lays and stares at the ceiling for a moment, studying the wood grain of the tree. She is deep in thought hoping that when she gets up she will hear Kora crashing about as she normally does when making her morning drink. She pauses for a moment longer and feels like something is amiss. She reaches to the stall beside her to pick up her shawl, wraps it around her shoulders and steps into the living area. Panic rushes over her when she realises the house is silent and Kora has not returned home.

She runs down the stairs sweeping through the bridges and down the spiralled staircases. She is heading straight for Nanuus house to see if Kora is there. When she discovers that Nanuu is home alone, she begins searching the forest floor calling Koras name. The elders hear her cries and demand her to tell them what has occurred. She informs them Kora has not returned home.

A loud horn echoes through the trees startling the villagers. Ailah looks at one of the elders faces and sees pure dread. It's the Ophiuchus.

The village is silent, the dwellers frozen in fear watching as Prince Daimon and his serpent guards march into the centre of the village on their Salamander beasts. All that can be heard is the thudding of the beasts feet on the ground and the clinking of the soldiers armour.

There is a long silence as Prince Daimon climbs down from his beast and stands looking around at these Libran creatures. He walks towards the elders and demands his betrothed be brought to him immediately.

"But sire, this is not the tradition of the treaty" one elder says sheepishly.

" I don't care for your traditions, bring me the girl NOW!" Shouts Daimon into the elders face.

" I'm afraid she is not here my lord" he says whilst cowering to his knees.

Ailah looks on in fear of what Daimon will do next.

Daimon is filled with rage, he draws his sword and stabs it slowly into the elders neck. He turns to his champion Seth and says "Kill them all but bring me her family and send some men to find her".

Smoke is filling the air as the homes are torched. Screams are carried along with the wind, howling through the trees as the Librans are being slaughtered. Ailah is flung into a cage and hits her head as she lands. Staring at the ground, all she can see is the ground flowing with blood, ash and fire. Nanuu is tied up, the soldiers tormenting her for being old and dumpy. She is pulled into the cage next to Ailah.

It is a sad day for the Librans.

CHAPTER NINE

We had escaped the city unharmed and spent the following nine days roaming the hills, searching for the next clue and avoiding capture of course. Boy! did I have a lot to teach this young lass! About her own city. Her own people. This little lady had been living in a bubble and did not know a thing about her history or the history of her kin. I mean, I told her some of it but, not before we met Crabby Ash, as I liked to call her. A funny old creature she was. She never did like my pet name. What we hadn't realised is that we had already circled it about ten thousand times in those nine days. We were lost and were giving up hope.

"Who goes there!?" a low and rumbling voice yelled

"Quick Kora! Get down!" Fynn yelled.

Kora crouched down into the marsh where Fynn laid to hide from the loud bellowing voice.

"It sounds like a giant," Kora whispered.

"They are," said Fynn. "They are the Cancerians, they are huge! And they aren't fussy about what or who they eat! I'm afraid we have stumbled into their territory."

"Can't you shift and hide us somehow before they find us?"

"Well no, not with this shackle still stuck around my arm."

Thud thud thud...

"I can smell you! Where are you?!...HA! Got you! There you are! HA!"...

The giant scooped Fynn and Kora up under its arm. Dangling upside down like poor defenceless animals about to be strung up and roasted over a fire.

"Here, Goronn, look what I found. What are they?"

"That's an Aquarian and that one...I'm not sure? Is it a Libran? I thought they were all dead Ash."

"Aargh!! Let us go! We are not your food!" squealed Kora

"It's talking Goronn, what's it want?"

"It wants you to put it down, Ash"

Ash squeezed a little harder, to be sure that she didn't drop them. She wanted to inspect these little beings, she was fascinated. Lucky for them, she wasn't hungry at all, being that she had only recently feasted. Kora scowled and hissed at her. The blue one was slightly larger than the red-haired one, less grumpy too. Her large pincers raised up from her underarms to prod at Kora and Fynn.

"What are you? What are you doing here?" She asked as she propped them down onto a rock.

Fynn and Kora looked up at this giant's face. It had similar features to theirs but was made of a hard shell. Speckled Brown, orange and cracked.

"We have just escaped Amoran and are on a quest to find something," said Fynn.

"What you looking for?"

"Well, we are looking for the pieces of the Libran staff that belonged to King Erald."

"Pah! That was a long time ago, how do you know it still exists?"

"Kora here had a vision, her goddess Hera told her to find it and so we shall. After many years of being a dogsbody, I want freedom! Will you join us Ash? Surely the Ophiuchus have done your kind wrong too?"

"Meh! I dunno, let me think about it, you should camp here for the night you both look a bit scrawny and famished! I'll tell some stories, I love stories."

Two hours later, the day star was setting. Kora and Fynn were huddled around a fire with full bellies listening to Ash tell her tales.

'Davanos could see that his journey had come to a victorious end. All his troubles were about to disappear with one fell swoop of his sword. He was about to save the city. All the teachings of his predecessors would be remembered and not burned away like the wicked witch Saskia the Serpent had promised. All creatures of this world would be saved. First, a quick glance towards his King for the nod of approval.

He swung his mighty weapon to unleash all of its remaining power on her. Remembering everything that had led up to this very moment'...

"Ash! That is enough with these old tales again, we have work to do! Come, help me clean up!"

"Oh but I love this one, even though it's got a horrid ending, I like this tale" Ash pleaded with Goronn.

"Oh, I guess I'll have to tell you the rest later, on our travels". Ash whispered as she winked and tucked blankets around them both. "Now, get some rest. I'll help Goronn and we will set off at daybreak".

CHAPTER TEN

Beta Librae began to rise the following morning. The crisp cool air of night slowly turned into a warm glow that Kora could feel on her cheeks as she stirred. She was so cosy considering they had slept by the fire all night and it had gone out. As she came to, she heard a grumble and realised that she was actually cuddled up to Fynn.

Bolting upright, feeling a little awkward, Kora sat and pondered the journey ahead. Smoke still coming away from the remains of the fire, she took a deep breath and could feel the smoke in her nostrils. She pulled the map and pendant from her satchel. Laying them both out on the dirt by her feet, she picked up the pendant to examine it and held it above the crumpled map. A flash of light burned a spot on the map and some letters appeared. The Taurean Mountains. She gasped.

So, that's how it works.

Just then, Fynn awoke from his slumber.

"Ah, good morning beautiful! What a glorious day it is!"

"Glorious?"

"Yes, Kora it is glorious! I am free and we did not become Ash and Goronn's dinner!" He chuckled.

"Look Fynn, we need to go to the Taurean Mountains. It's only about half a days walk from here." Kora said as she pointed to the map.

"Well, we best be off then. Let's wake Ash and then be on our way."

"Morning you two, are you ready? Here, Fynn let me help you with that band on your arm." Ash said sincerely as she snipped away the metal with her solid pincer.

"Wow! Thanks! I thought I would never be rid of that thing! We can get there a lot faster now! Look, I'll show you what I can do!" Kora and Ash looked on in amazement and began giggling as Fynn was shifting and swirling around laughing and yelling with pure glee. Transforming into all different creatures.

"Stand still I will grab you both, you may get a bit wet." Fynn bellowed as he transformed into a giant water horse and scooped them both up. He was so fast. Kora couldn't really understand how this was working or what she was holding onto.

Whipping through fields and over hills, she began to see the mountain creep up over the horizon. She could feel her cheeks moving uncontrollably, he was going that fast.

"Oh no! Look it's the serpent soldiers! They are chasing us! They must have spotted us!" screamed Ash.

Fynn was fast but they were catching up very quickly. He spun to the right and headed into a nearby forest crashing through the bushes and thistles. Kora squealed as Fynn leapt through them not realising the thorns had scraped her leg badly. They quickly found a tunnel covered with ivy, so they hid for a short while until they were sure they had lost the serpents.

In a panic, they rush deeper and deeper into the wood. Until Kora yells at the others to stop. "Wait! I need to stop for a moment!" She said as she sat on a stump trying to catch her breath, her skin stinging from the branches slicing as they whipped her body.

"I think we lost them but we are not alone in this wood," Fynn said with a look of worry on his face. He turns to see a sharp arrow pointing centimetres away from his eye, the archer ready to take the shot.

"Nope not alone," he mumbles.

"Who are you and what are you doing in the Sagittarian quarter?" demanded one of the soldiers that surrounded them.

Before giving the friends a chance to answer the soldiers swiftly marched them into the Sagittarian castle to await sentencing for trespassing.

"Let us go!" screeches Kora as she tries desperately to fight off the soldiers holding her.

"We were just hiding from the serpents until we knew the coast was clear to continue onto The Taurean Mountains! We did not mean to trespass!"

A deafening horn goes off and silence befalls the grand hall that they were being held in. Kora glances around in a panic noticing the white limestone and marble pillars, engraved and embossed with what must be the Sagittarian symbol, a bow, and an arrow. Looking towards the front of the room, she notices a female walking down the steps at the center. Wearing a dark green hooded cape she gracefully glides towards Kora. Her face lights up and she draws nearer and realizes who Kora is. She looked a bit like an elf from one of Nanuu's old tales. Tall and slim with long chestnut brown hair and pointy ears.

"Oh, the day has come! Release them immediately!"

"But your grace? They were trespassing!"

"I said to release them! This is the young Libran! I foresaw this, she is the key to defeating the serpents" The Oracle demanded firmly.

"Come, young lady, we will dine and I will tell you what I know."

The Oracle guides them through the hall and out onto a terrace, walls decorated with blankets of ivy, a grand table and stone chairs with high backs, they look like thrones. A feast of fruits, vegetables, meats, and bread laid out across the table.

"This feast could feed the whole Libran tribe."Kora thought to herself.

"Oh yum, Food! I'm starving!" Ash rushed to the biggest chair that she could find and tucked right in.

"Forgive me, let me introduce myself properly, my name is Luna and I am the Sagittarian Oracle. I serve as a ruler to my people after the serpents killed our Lord Sagitari. Kora, I must tell you, I knew your parents. Such wonderful people, they were dear friends of mine."

"My parents? I'm sorry your grace I don't really remember them or know much about them really. They died when I was a babe. I was raised by my Aunt Ailah."

"Oh Darling, I know that they are no longer with us. I must tell you that Ailah is not your true aunt either. She was tasked with protecting you and raising you. Keeping you away from the serpents. Your parents were the King and Queen of Hera you see. The Libran King Erald is your father. The reason you look differently to most Libran's is because you are of royal blood. When they realised that they would suffer defeat they had you whisked away into the forest for your own protection. In the hope that one day, you would be told who you really are and what you must do for justice."

" I don't understand? I have been betrothed to one of them. That is why I sought advice from the Goddess Hera,"

" Yes, well your tribe's elders were pressured into a deal. They must not have known who you were, Ailah would have taken an oath and been sworn to secrecy. They offer up a certain number of girls every year to the serpents in order for the rest of the tribe to survive, what they do with those girls I'm not sure of, no one knows. A lot of the species that call this place home have similar arrangements. The Saggitarians do not have an arrangement though, when we were defeated we fled here to what is now known as the Sagittarian quarter. We keep to the forest and usually shoot down any trespassers. See, the serpents killed their own planet, sucked it dry of all resources. They then travelled to different constellations to invade. They captured slaves and then finally arrived here on the Libran planet Hera and were victorious."

Kora is filled with frustration and anger at the thought of being lied to, her entire life. She understands that it was for good reason but it still hurts a lot.

'How could they keep the truth from me?'

"So Kora is a Princess?" asked Fynn.

"Well, no Kora is not a princess but she is, in fact, the Libran Queen of Hera. She became queen the day her parents were tragically taken from us. Of course, you will need a formal coronation, but not before we defeat the serpents."

Kora sat astounded and speechless at what she had just heard. She almost felt like the oracle was about to tell her that she was just kidding around.

"Me? A normal forest dweller? Queen of the Librans? Is this why the goddess sent me on this journey."

"Oh you are far from normal Kora and what did your goddess tell you to do?" Luna chuckled.

"We are helping Kora find the staff of Amoran. We need to get to the Taurean Mountains." Garbled Ash as she continued to stuff her face with more food.

"Ah, that's not far from here. But, be warned, it's not a very friendly place. I will send two of my best soldiers, Kobi and Omah, with you to help. You can sleep here tonight and leave at first light."

The following morning the friends set off towards the Taurean Mountains along with the soldiers on horseback. As they were leaving the Oracle rushed over to Kora and placed a blue star-shaped gem into her palm.

"Here, you will need this, it is a part of the Staff. I kept it safe for you."

Kora slipped the gem into her satchel as the horse began to trot and turned back to thank the Oracle, it almost looked like a throwing star, it had a hole right through the middle. The path that led out of the forest reminded her of home. The smell of moss and lagoon water, the sounds of plants tapping and clicking away and the colours, the vibrant and blinding colours.

"Oh, I wish I could bathe in the lagoon right now" Kora sighed and turned to Fynn."

"I don't need to bathe Kora, I am water, I can be a lagoon for you though" He chuckled and galloped off as he shifted into a stallion.

"Very funny" she mumbled, a little embarrassed at the thought of Fynn seeing her bare skin.

After a while of travelling towards the mountains. They could see the biggest one drawing closer and closer. The path and its surroundings turned from flowers and life to soil and stone. The silence was deafening. All that could be heard was the gentle gallop of the horses and the occasional splashing from Fynn. They all grew slightly nervous but were determined and ready for anything to happen. The path grew steeper as they began to climb the mountain.

"Why are they called The Taurean mountains?" Kora asked.

One of the soldiers, Omah turned to her and said "Because it's where the Taurean lives and roams. No creature has ever dared to go near the mountain through fear of being crushed or trampled except the odd Ophiuchus... who would never return. He guards the staff. He does not care for visitors and charges at them. He is half a bull after all."

58

"Why is he alone up there?"

"A lot of his people died in the Taurean war on their planet Aphrodite and those that remained were taken to other places to serve as slaves for the Ophiuchus. He was brought to Hera, managed to escape the serpents and sought refuge with King Erald. He was given a part of the Staff to take to the mountain and guard for your arrival. But, his years of solitude have filled him with madness and sorrow. I cannot think of a worse form of torture than to live in solitude for the rest of my days. It will not be an easy task to acquire the staff. We must creep quietly past and hope that he does not spot us. It would be a pity to have to kill the only living Taurean on Hera" followed Kobi.

As they grew nearer to the top, they got down from the horses and tied them up. They would need to climb the rest of the way on foot.

"The coast seems clear. Maybe he's not here anymore?"

"I hope not. I'm getting tired now, all this climbing! Cancerians aren't made for climbing!" moaned Ash as she huffed, puffed and let out a big sigh.

They reached the top a little tired and achy but otherwise unscathed to immediately be thrown into a battle and trying to evade capture. The serpents were waiting for them. It was an ambush.

Ash charged towards them like a mountain lion, roaring and knocking them down with a swipe of her pincers. Kobi and Omah began circling the mountain top shooting them down, one by one, with arrows. Fynn rushed towards the last soldiers and began swirling around them like a tornado.

"Run Kora! Get the staff! I will hold them off!" he yelled.

Kora squeaked and ran as fast as she could diving towards the staff like a frightened little mouse and grabbing it as she fell to the ground. Eyes welling up as she got to her feet again angry at herself for being frightened. Ash grabbed the soldiers and began flinging them from the mountain top. One slipped away and retreated. Scurrying off down the mountain as fast as he could.

Kora looked at the staff again. It was missing the top part. It was just a wooden stick with some gems on the shaft. Hands still shaking she gripped her new trophy tightly.

"Maybe the gem that The Oracle gave me will fit on to the top." Kora thought as she lifted it up. "It does! But, it's still missing something. A hole, maybe another stone sits there and..." Kora paused with sudden realisation... "the handle of my bone dagger is part of it as well."

"Er, guys, we've got company," said Fynn rather nervously as he swooped down and shifted back into his usual form.

"What are you doing on my mountain!" A voice roared and rumbled the stones on the ground. The coast wasn't clear.

"Run!"

Fynn splashed and shifted into a pack of wild horses and scooped everyone up. He swooped down the mountain as fast as he could, Tor chased them yelling, eyes glowing with anger until he had grown bored and given up the chase. He was an old bull now. Not as energetic as he once was. His brown fur and ripped muscles had turned grey and frail.

"Well, that was close! It could have been a lot quicker and easier for you to splash up there and get it Fynn rather than making me climb all the way up there!" Ash groaned.

"Well where's the fun in that?" laughed Fynn.

CHAPTER ELEVEN

Kora is gripping the staff tightly and studying it, she notices some parchment wrapped around the bottom and unravels it. It is a letter addressed to her.

> *My Darling Kora,*
>
> *If you are reading this*
>
> *I am glad because it means you are on the right path.*
>
> *Take the staff and go to the Scorpion Realm,*
>
> *You must earn their trust and loyalty.*
>
> *Trust me in telling you they are worthy allies*
>
> *to have and you will need their*
>
> *assistance if you are to liberate Hera.*
>
> *With love From,*
>
> *Your Father King Erald.*

Kora is tearful as she folds the letter and places it into her satchel. She turns to Fynn and says "we need to go to the Scorpion Realm, the letter was from my father and it says that's where we need to go next".

Fynn looks at Kora and says "Scorpion Realm? That doesn't sound like a lot of fun, I will check the map on how to get there".

Kora passes him the pendant and the map, he places the map on the ground and dangles the pendant above it. A flash of light passes through it and burns the next spot on the map.

"We have to go south to the water and cross the ocean to get to the Scorpion realm. We will pass through Piscean Territory."

Kora suddenly remembers the Goddess Hera telling her to collect a siren stone from the maiden of the sea.

Three days later, the treacherous storms and waves slapping against the ramshackled boat were enough to put Kora off from continuing this tiresome journey. She thought that really it could have been easier to stay ashore and let Fynn handle this one alone. Kora felt that she could rest a little knowing that the next task lay in her trusted friend and allies hands. See, Fynn would be the one to take lead on this quest as he could breathe underwater and hopefully communicate with whatever creature guarded the Siren Stone. She was relying on him.

Once connected to her mighty staff it would rain justice down on the wicked serpents in battle.

They had been floating around the islands in the water for what had felt like days whilst Kobi and Omah had stayed ashore to fight off any serpents that came by and tried to halt their endeavours. Searching for a sign of the siren stone. The map said they were on the right spot, but all that could be seen anywhere nearby was sea, the odd bird flying past, sea and more sea. Starving and weary, they were ready to fold. Ash even shed a tear for her poor rumbling tummy.

"Wait? What is that sound?" Fynn hushed his comrades.

"I don't hear nothing, except my poor tum!" said Ash

"You wouldn't, you are almost as deaf as a doorknob crabby, and clearly too hungry to think straight." Fynn teased.

"It's beautiful, What is it?! It's coming from underneath us in the water! I'm going in!"

Before his friends could even process and acknowledge what Fynn had just said he was gone, and they were soaked from his dive. The bitter salt water filled Kora's mouth. Disgusting.

He followed the sweet sounds deep, deep into the ocean. The singing got louder and louder. He could not see where it was coming from. The water had grown very dark and murky.

Suddenly, a gust of bubbles and froth circled him. Spinning around and around like a tornado.

Whack! Something hit him and made him woozy.

'Well, that was unexpected.' he thought as he shook it off.

Whatever it was felt like a giant club or bat. Glancing around still a little dazed to see the creature staring back at him as if it were observing whether he was a threat or not.

As he gained a little of his strength back, and the sea stopped spinning he managed to mutter the word "Hello". He realised that this creature before him was a Siren. Others knew them as Pisceans and she had clumped him with her tail.

He studied this creature just as she observed him. Her long locks of hair appeared as if it were made of black pearls.

"Who are you? What are you doing here?" the siren demanded.

"The names Fynn. I am an Aquarian. I'm here with my friends to find the Siren stone."

"I am Pearl, a Pisces maiden of the sea. Protector of the Siren stone and my kin. Why do you seek the stone?"

Well... my friend Kora she is a Libran, the daughter of King Erald and has been tasked with finding the staff of Amoran by the Goddess Hera. In order for us to take back our freedom from the Ophiuchus and the stone is one of the final pieces to the weapon.``

"Just you? Where is your battalion of warriors for this rebellion?"

"We don't have one yet. Once we have retrieved the staff, we will build our army. The creatures of this planet will have hope as we will show them that they can be free again"

"Well, I must ask for something in return before I allow you to take the siren stone. If you succeed in retrieving an item for my people then I shall consider it. I would also like to meet Kora, daughter of King Erald. Then I and my people will fight by your side," Pearl stated sincerely.

"Come with me to the seabed. I will show you where we live and tell you of the item we require."

"Excuse me, miss Pearl? If you don't mind me asking? How can you fight by our side on land? Do the serpents come into the water now? I did not think the port had been completed yet..." Fynn asked.

"We can dwell on land too but this will only happen if you retrieve the item, we are sirens after all. We choose to stay in the water because not only is it our home but the serpents cannot defeat or control us in this form. However, we need a magical orb that is hidden in the frozen ice caverns of Grimgarde. It is in the Windshell ocean south of here. We would retrieve it ourselves but I'm afraid we cannot swim in those waters. The Ophiuchus have cursed it with some dark magic and it poisons any Piscean that dares to try. We will fight by your side on the battleground though once we can use the orb. We have waited long for this day. The serpents have been trying to starve and poison us out of the sea for a lifetime now. They must be stopped."

The dive downward grew murkier and murkier until suddenly it was crystal clear. Fynn looked ahead at the coral reef palace that sat before him. He was in awe.

"Oh, I wish I could have a home like that!"

The tropical fish swimming around lighting up the way. Sea plants whistling tunes just like the plants Kora had talked about in the Libra Forest. This place had remained untouched by the serpents. Everywhere else there was evidence of death and destruction.

"Come on then, I know it's pretty but I don't have all day." Pearl urged as she floated off towards the doorway that resembled a giant cave opening. Tiny fish and sea creatures glowing and lighting the room up. It is beautiful. Fynn followed Pearl into what must have been the underwater throne room, only the thrones were around a large circular table made from glittering seashells and the thrones were brightly coloured coral. Pearl swam towards one and floated down to sit on it gently, it seemed as though it was alive. She went on to explain to Fynn that the task she had given him did not come without risks and the potential of serious harm to Fynn and his friends.

"There are deadly creatures in those waters, so you must be careful" she advised.

Pearl explained that Fynn and his friends must go to the cavern and break down the ice barrier that is warded with magic and for this they would need the support of the Scorpios. "It is their magic that seals it," she said.

Meanwhile, Kora and Ash were facing a problem. The ram shackled boat had started to sink. Fynn must have been keeping them afloat somehow. Desperately splashing around, they were trying to stay above water.

"Oh, No Kora! I can't swim!"

"But Ash, You're a Cancerian? Aren't crabs part sea creature."

"Not this one Kora, I've never been in the water!"

Just as the boat totally submerged Fynn appeared and lifted it back up.

"What are you two doing? Goofing around? While I'm on an important mission?" he said with a tone like he was extremely proud of himself.

"Very funny waterboy" Ash fired back.

"Did you find the siren stone?"

"Yes...well...about that... I may have agreed to an extra mission and found an army to fight with us. The Pisceans want to meet you but not before we retrieve an orb for them from the Ice caverns of Grimgarde".

"Grimgarde? That's days away Fynn?" cried Ash.

"Yes ... but a necessary detour...after we have been to the Scorpion realm of course as we need their magic too".

"So that's the Sagittarians and now the Pisceans that will stand by our side? Providing we get this Orb for them? " Kora asked.

"Yes but we must also try to save my people, the Aquarians, and try to rally more troops, it will not be easy." Fynn stopped and stared into the distance, sparing a moment to think of his friends back in the city. He worried for them. He worried for all of the Aquarians.

'Now that the serpents know that I have escaped and am helping Kora they will be in true danger.'

"I'll get the Cancerians on board, hopefully Goronn has found them by now, I will go home and get them to come with me to meet you all in the Sagittarian quarter."

CHAPTER TWELVE

One week later, Kora and her friends are heading toward the most western hemisphere of Hera after regrouping at the Sagittarian Quarter. They had reached the desert, the outer border of the scorpion realm. Kora could feel the sharp sand slip between her toes and spray backward as she walked her horse through the sea of golden lava. It burned the soles of her feet and whipped her legs, the day star was heating the ground to the point where it felt like a furnace. She grit her teeth and pressed on ignoring the pain and stinging as she needed to give her horse a break from being mounted.

The air on the horizon looked as if it were melting but for the first time in days Kora thought she could see something in the distance. She could see some trees.

"Shade!" she cried out to her friends with a dry and croaky voice as she pointed in the direction of the trees.
"Ah, yes that must be the edge of the Scorpion Realm" said Omah.
"Lets go and rest under the shade of the trees and rest the horses for a while"

Reaching the trees felt like a huge achievement after the torturous journey that Kora and her friends had just endured. Fynn thought he would evaporate at one point. She threw herself down under the tree after leading her horse to the shade and checked the soles of her feet. Rubbing them a little in the hope that the pain would go away. Leaning her back on the rough bark and pressing her feet into the cool ground she felt utterly exhausted but grateful to be alive.

"How far is it from here do you think? Said Ash.

"I will check the map" Kora croaked as she pulled it from her satchel. Just as she stood up and turned toward the tree to observe the map she noticed a glint in the distance. Something reflecting the day stars light.

She stepped past the trees trying to get a better view of what it was while her friends all laid on the ground sprawled out. Kobe looked up and saw Kora wondering off and followed her.

"Kora" he called out.

She turned back and looked at him. "What do you think that is?" she pointed to the thing glinting in the distance.

"That must be the Scorpion Palace, they have glass mirrors to decorate the outer walls and create reflections. The mirrors are also magic somehow but you'll have to ask the Scorpios how they work."

As they reached the steps of the desert city they were greeted with hostility. The Scorpios stood to attention with their magical spears ready to strike. Kora carefully revealed the staff to them that had been hanging from the side of her saddle.

"My name is Kora, I am here to seek support from your leaders" she declared to the guards as she held up the staff. "I come on behalf of the Librans and all of the Zodiacs that have been dominated and enslaved by the Ophiuchus" she continued.

She paused for a moment and looked around at her friends and then back to the guards who did not move a muscle. It is as if they are statues frozen to the spot.

"Where did you get that staff girl?" a voice questioned from above.
Kora looked up to see that she did have an audience after all hoping that whoever it was would not notice that the siren stone is missing. A balcony with a terrace sat directly above the steps held up by gold leaf and glass pillars.

"I was tasked with finding it and piecing it together by the goddess Hera" she replied.
"I was advised to come here to the Scorpion Realm by my father, the Libran King Erald.." just as Kora went on to explain further the creatures bellowed down to her.
"LIES! The Libran King has been dead for years..."
"I know he is dead, please if you would let me explain...when I found the staff it had a letter with it addressed to me...from my father advising me to seek the support of the Scorpios.
"Ah well..why didn't you just say that" the voice chuckled as he leaned over the side and signalled to the guard to stand down and let Kora and her friends pass.

Fynn walked quickly up to Kora and whispered to her "wow, you sounded like a true royal then. Getting used to the idea now are we? Your highness..."he sniggered.

Kora rolled her eyes at him and gave her friends a nod and began to walk forward through the large doorway. The cool air hit their faces as they walked through into a courtyard. As they came to a standstill they looked around the courtyard and noticed all of the scorpios watching them...staring and waiting.

Kora felt uneasy and gripped the staff a little tighter. The silence was deafening for a while. A scorpio then entered through a doorway to the right and ushered the audience away. Once everyone was out of the way an old fellow stepped through a door to the left.

"So...you are the daughter of the King?" he asked.

"Can you prove it?" He continued.

"How can I prove it to you sir? I did not know who my parents were until recently" said Kora.

"That does not matter girl. If you pass this test then it will give me the truth I seek".

He places four objects on the stone pillars in front of Kora and directs her to choose only one. A carved blue diamond, a clay jug of water, a dying flower and the final object is a golden bracelet.

She stands and observes the objects for a moment peering briefly at the jug of water and then over at the dying flower. She steps toward the diamond filled with temptation and reaches out but hesitates as her hand gets near to the jewel. Something inside her tells her to break the rules and choose more than one object. Nervously, she picks up the jug of water looking up at the Scorpio whose eyes are staring through her with anticipation. Kora gulps and steps toward the flower, pouring the water onto it.

The water glows like magic and feeds life to the flower.

The Scorpio chuckles softly and grins. "Congratulations Kora, you have passed the test. Many would give in to temptation and take the jewels or gold but you chose to give life and support to a being that needed it. If you had chosen the other objects you would have been cursed"

Just as the Scorpio finishes a bug lands on the diamond and the friends watch the life drain from its carcass. Fynn shudders and quietly mumbles under his breath "phew, so glad that bug wasn't Kora".

She looks on and waits for the Scorpio's next move studying him closely. He wears a brown leather cape on the upper half of his body much like an old and frail Libran man but when Kora looks down she sees that he has the legs and tail of a scorpion. As he moves slowly toward her she notices that his silver-white beard drapes down to his chest and it's glowing un-naturally.

"Right this way" he says as he bows down and points to where Kora and her friends need to go.

They slowly walk through a brick tunnel, the light so dim that they can barely see the way. They reach a door braced with iron and a lock that looks like it would be impossible to break. The Scorpio gave a flick of the wrist, whispering a spell and the door begins to unlock. As the door opens a flood of light fills the tunnel and dazzles Kora. Fynn squeals "I see the light" and the friends laugh.

The Scorpio is not amused at Fynn's remark and walks off ahead hurrying the friends along. They reach an altar where a group of Scorpio Lords sit around in a circle waiting for their arrival. The old Scorpio introduces Kora to them and informs them that she has passed the test before giving a nod and disappearing.

"So you are Kora?" one of the lords asks rhetorically.

Ash takes this the wrong way and spitefully hisses "well you're not much of a hotshot now are yo…" Kora interrupts Ash and apologises saying "What my friend means is... Yes I am Kora'' as she looks back at Ash with a disapproving look on her face.

"I am the supreme ruler of the Scorpion Realm. My name is Lord Dondor and this is Lord Sansai and Lord Elfard." He pauses looking a little bemused.

Fynn turns to his friends and mutters " I think it is so strange how they all have the same first name,,,Lord? It's not even a good one."

"What is it you seek?" Lord Dondor says as he looks at them very confused.

"I seek the support of the Scorpion Realm. We must fight back against the Ophiuchus." Kora begins her speech.

"Why should we help you young Libran? Yes you passed the test for entrance but what will you do for us in return?" Lord Dondor states.

He gets up and begins to pace the forecourt deep in thought for a moment "We have been at war with the Ophiuchus for a very long time. Our resources on Hera are dwindling. They keep interrupting our efforts when scouting for the items that we need. If you find a way to defeat those Ophiuchus at the outpost that is north of the desert and free my Scorpio kin that they have kept prisoner there, then and only then will the scorpion realm support your efforts for rebellion".

A few hours later , Kora and her companions are rested, given supplies and begin making their way to the outpost to free the Scorpios.

"Errr, question. How are the five of us gonna defeat a whole load of serpents at the outpost?" Ash abruptly asks.

Omah looks at her and says "well, that is something we need to consider Ash".

"We need to each use our gifts in some way, besides my good looks and charm, you all know I can shift". Fynn says proudly while posing with his hands on his hips and his chest puffed out.

Kora smirks at him, then looking around at her friends she agrees and says " Fynn is right. Ash you can use your mighty strength, Kobe and Omar you are magnificent archers and can move as fast as the wind but quieter. So we have

an element of surprise. Fynn you can flood them you know with your charm,oops
I mean water. And I can bring the plants to life".

Giggling at her clever response to his remark Fynn states "That is a great
plan Your Royalness".

They are nearing the outpost nervous about what will unfold beyond the wall.
It's late, the moonlight is filling the sky, the sparkling stars twinkling
with an abundance of colours. It's slumber time for many of the serpents and
it's quiet beyond the gate as far as they can tell. Kora looks up at it's
beauty then turns to her comrades and whispers "are you ready?".They all nod
in agreement.

Once they reach the large wooden gate, bolted with iron and rusted metal. Kora
glances at Kobe and Omah and whispers " now". As fast as she could blink they
were gone, each going in a different direction to silently scan the perimeter
for lookouts. Kobe finds one, sneaks up behind him, grabs him and cuts his
throat with his dagger.

Meanwhile, Omah is the other side, he's stopped and is waiting and almost
camouflaged into the desert foliage, he shoots the serpent and rushes to grab
him to avoid a large thud from the fall. He pulls his Ophiuchus victim behind
a mound of sandstones and heads back to Kora.

Kora is waiting eagerly for Omahs return, Kobe has cleared his side. He
returns and taps Ash on the shoulder, giving her the go ahead. She crashes

through the gate, her shell-like body protecting her as an amour. She bursts through, serpent soldiers beyond the gate begin to panic, rushing around for their weapons.

Ash fights off three serpents with one mighty swoop of her pincers flinging them into the air. Fynn begins to shift, creating a whirlpool tsunami drowning many of the Ophiuchus soldiers that are now fighting back. Kora finds some cacti and spins sharp vines covered with needle-like thorns and traps them with her botanical power. Kobi and Omah release the Scorpios and gather them outside the gate.

They kill every serpent soldier at the outpost except for one. Kora angrily says "tell your leader his time is almost over of reigning destruction on my planet, you'll have to find your own way out of those shackles first though".

Back at the Scorpion City, Kora and her friends are being celebrated for saving the imprisoned Scorpios. A Banquet has filled their tummies, Ash has eaten for hours. The Scorpio Lords are sitting at the centre table with Kora, Ash, Fynn, Kobe and Omah. Lord Dondor stands and turns to his scorpion servant who taps a golden spoon upon a crystal glass. Silence befalls the room, the guards stand to attention around the decadent hall. "I, Lord Dondor, want to tell you all that a new age is coming. The chosen one is here. Kora, you have completed what was an impossible task to free our kin with your comrades and we are eternally grateful. We the Scorpios will be your allies and help you take back Hera and defeat the Ophiuchus"

CHAPTER THIRTEEN

Two days later they are fast approaching ice caverns of Grimgarde, they have ten Scorpio soldiers with them. They are armed with silver swords cast from spells and minerals from the planet. They reach a frozen lake, Kora watches in hope as the soldiers circle it and simultaneously stab their swords into the ice. They move them in a circular motion and deeply chant getting louder and louder.

"Ice of stone, ice of poison, release your curse to free the maiden, Ice of stone, ice of poison, release your curse to free the maiden, Ice of stone, ice of poison, release your curse to free the MAIDEN!".

Fynn swoops into the water armed with a sword the Scorpio gifted him. He swims and swims for what feels like hours but it's minutes in reality. He sees something coming at him, a giant eel-like creature with teeth like jagged glass, eyes red with rage and scales as big as bird wings. He dodges it's bite and stabs it through the heart. The lake goes red with blood Kora starts to panic upon the lake shore. Fynn continues on; he swims further and spots the cavern, he can see a glow. He realises it's the orb and picks up his speed. He swoops it up and swims back to the lakeshore. He's exhausted, the water is icy and beginning to re freeze, Kobe reaches in and pulls out his aquarian friend. Fynn passes the orb to Kora and cheekily says while shivering " next time you need me to be a hero can you choose a warmer water temperature, my oracles nearly turned to icicles".

Kora laughs at her friend and says " well, I can't promise that but thanks to you, we now can take this to the Pisceans and get the siren stone".

A few sunrises later, Kora and her small battalion are out at sea again only this time the boat is larger. A ship built for war crafted by the Pisceans and left at the shore for the rebels to use to reach the territory. Waves lapping calmly, they look into the water over the boat edge. Fish glowing and guiding their journey to the Maiden.

Siren song echoes, this time they all hear the beautiful harmony. Pearl rises and behind her fifty or so Piscean sirens, they are waiting and watching for Fynn to bring them the Orb. He dives in and swoops to her, passes her the orb and says " I hope this means we still have you as allies and that we can retrieve the siren stone". She nods and passes him a glassy blue gem. He returns to Kora who is ready with the other pieces. She places the siren stone into the holes. As the sirens and scorpions, Ash, Kobe, Omah and Fynn watch in amazement, a beam of purple light shoots into the air like a comet.

The siren song is bellowing as they enter the water until they disappear fully submerged. Kora turns to Fynn and her friends filled with relief and states " we did it, we have the staff of Amoran. Now we reign justice down on the Ophiuchus and free the Zodiacs".

CHAPTER FOURTEEN

'We must stay quiet.' Kobi whispers and waves the battalion of twenty soldiers towards the wood at the foot of Amoran city. It is sundown and the Aquarians will all have been herded back to their cells by now. The Cancerians with their heavy shells are clunking along trying to be as quiet as they can, hushing one another as they go. Ash and her kin are the keys to freeing the Aquarians by snipping off their shackles and releasing their power to shift.

Kora had stayed behind with Luna to prepare for the rebellion with the remaining troops and learn about her past. As much as Luna can tell her anyway.

"Fynn, you will need to guide us through to the cells." he continued.

"Ash you will then free them and we can try and get as many out as possible before alerting anyone."

"Right, got it, stay quiet and free the Aquarians. Wouldn't mind crushing a few serpent skulls though" Ash retorted.

"Well your wish will most definitely be granted, they are everywhere all the time. This will be impossible to get them out without a fight," said Fynn.

They begin sneaking up and slipping over the wall, silently taking out the soldiers that were on guard. Fynn guiding them through the streets to the cells. The soldier in there with the key is quickly silenced by Omah, a swift slice to the throat from behind, he then cleans his blade and stealthily creeps forward. They begin unlocking the doors and pulling them open as quietly as possible.

"Quickly and silently everyone! Follow us! We are getting you out of here!" He demands.

Ash and Goronn begin snipping away at the shackles around their arms and hurrying them out the door.

They move from cell to cell freeing as many as they can until they hear the deafening sound of a horn. The serpents are aware of the intrusion and begin flooding into the courtyard.

"Hold them off! We have one more cell to do!" Ash yelled.

Kobi, Omah, the Saggitarians, and Cancerians begin fighting them off viciously. Chopping, hacking and slashing away.

Meanwhile, Fynn has slipped into the tower and up to the abandoned throne room. Luna had told him of some armour there that would be perfect for Kora in battle. He grabbed it from one of the chests at the foot of the shelving inset into the walls and flew back down to join the others.

"Faster Goronn! Faster!" Ash pleaded.

"Alright, I'm going as fast as I can! five, four, three, two...one! Next cell!"

Ash and Goronn ripped the door open and freed the Aquarians as quickly as they could. They swooped into the courtyard and began flinging soldiers about like rag-dolls.

"Ouch! That one tried to stab me with its dory!" Goronn yelled as he picked it up and threw it at the wall as hard as he could. The Aquarians begin shifting and transforming all as one into a giant wall of water. Blocking the soldiers from their rescuers.

They stayed put until Ash and the others had escaped and then splashed down the wall like a giant wave. The serpents no longer had Aquarian slaves. Once they were all out of harm's way and far from the city. Fynn yelled out with pure joy. He was ecstatic that finally with the help of his friends, he had finally freed his people.

CHAPTER FIFTEEN

As Kora approaches her chambers after a long day of deliberating with her council members she begins to tremble. The room has grown dim and there is a chill in the air. The fire has not yet been lit. The heavy wooden door creaks as it closes slowly behind her and clicks loudly as it shuts. Finally, she is alone. She had been passed a crumpled note earlier on by one of the scouts that had been out looking for the Librans hoping for some good news about her family.

She unfolds the crumpled parchment and drops to her knees in sorrow as she reads it and discovers that Daimon has Ailah and Nanuu as prisoners. He had ransacked the village and killed many of the villagers when he discovered that Kora had left the village. The impact of the cold, hard tile against her knees sent a sharp pain through her body but she did not care about the pain. The grief had overtaken. She knelt for hours wailing and sobbing, endless tears streaming down her delicate cheeks. Her planet was dying. Her home would be lost. Her kin have suffered because of her.

She had tried to remain strong and calm in front of everyone but when she was alone, as rare as that was now that she was Queen, she would crumble.

The pain and heaviness of heart were almost too much to bear, she could feel it coursing through her body, the unwanted feelings pulsing through her veins, from the tips of her toes to the tips of her fingers.

Questions remaining unanswered spinning in her mind, making her feel dizzy.

'Why are they doing this? Why are they killing Hera?'

Eventually, Kora crawled slowly toward her bed. Her body feels drained and bruised. She mustered the energy to creep up onto the bed and laid on top of the furs and pillows, curled like a baby in the fetal position, rocking back and forth and staring in solemn
thought until eventually, she drifted off to sleep.

A loud knocking at the door startled Kora as she woke. Rubbing her eyes and bolting upright she called out that she was coming.

"Yes? Who is it?" she said as she walked toward the door.

"It's me." the voice called through.
She instantly recognised Fynn's voice and opened the door to let him in forcing a pained smile.

"I just wanted to invite you to dinner, Kora. I couldn't find you in the quarter anywhere and was told that you had retired to your room with a sad look on your face? Are you ok?".

"I just feel like I am not strong enough. I am not the leader everyone wants me to be. I wish things could be simpler. Daimon the Ophiuchus prince has my family" Kora cries out as she begins to shed a tear.

"It hurts, it all hurts so much".

Fynn paused for a moment and looked at his friend remembering how much they had been through together. He put his hand on her shoulder and whispered sincerely "you are the strongest creature I know. Look at how far we have come. If it wasn't for you, then I would still be in shackles. You saved me. You have saved so many of us. Listen to me, we will get through this. You need to be strong. We need to have a plan. We will get them back".
He paused for a moment further as he wiped a tear from her cheek and gently brushed his hand down to her chin.

"I have an idea. But, it's risky" he said.

"Go on?" Kora looked up at him in anticipation.

"Well, we could trick them into thinking that we have surrendered."

" and… I could free my family from behind enemy lines?" Kora added.

Fynn looked at Kora and saw a spark of determination in her eye.
'There she is' he thought as he smiled sincerely.

Kora begins to pace, planning and plotting how she will do this and be successful in her efforts to free Ailah and Nanuu.

"Fynn will you go and see what information you can gather? Get a visual on the city and report back to me? I would like to know what I'm walking into before I do this".

"Certainly" he said as he got up to head out. He turned around, bowed and saluted to his queen and then walked off down the hall leaving Kora to prepare herself for dinner.

A few hours later, the door swings open, Kora turns and sees Kobi and a foot soldier holding another creature. A boy...

"What is going on? Who is this boy?" Kora demands.

"He says he's here for you, your grace. We found him trespassing the wood. He is a Virgo."

"A Virgo?" Kora questions as she looks into the boy's eyes. She can see they are filled with fear and trauma.

"Release him... what happened to you boy?"

"My name is Art, your grace, my companions and I escaped our settlement but we were caught by the serpents and they slaughtered everyone. They only let me go so that I can find you. They said to pass the message miss. That they are ready and waiting" Art says as he bows his head and begins to weep.

"My boy, we already defeated them at the Virgo settlement and freed as many Virgo as we possibly could."

"Well, you are safe now Art. Someone get this boy some food and a bed." Kora orders whilst turning toward the table. She begins pacing. Deciding to let the boy rest and recuperate before getting any more information from him.

'They taunt me, how infuriating. They must believe that I'm a true threat then. Good.'

Soaring through the clouds like a giant eagle Fynn took in a deep breath and looked at the beautiful views before him. His wings spread wide across the clouds like the white foam lapping against the shore. The planet Hera was his home now, had been for years. He needed to save her. Kora needed his help and so did everyone else.

Glancing to his left and gazing upon his friend Ostara flying elegantly through the mist of the clouds, filling with happiness and pride that he had helped to save her from a life of torment and terror.

'We are free, but the fight isn't over' he thought.

To his right, Cedrick was soaring through, twisting and turning, flying in loops. He was ecstatic and had a new lease of life. He had been shackled for so long that he thought he had forgotten how to be himself. How to shift, how to fly.

The sky was growing darker as they got closer to the city. It was not night time though, it was something else. The largest of the Ophiuchus vessels hovered above the city, casting a shadow that stretched for miles. Horrified they continued on to get a closer look. Flying higher and higher until they could see the true horror of what lay before them.

There were too many vessels to count. A sea of serpent soldiers are on the ground and grouped together in legions awaiting their commands. Thousands of them pouring out of the city and in the fields and valleys surrounding it. The vessels strategically docked in a grid-like form. The largest of them are still hovering above.

"We need to go back and warn the others!" he yelled out as he circled around and flew off into the distance.

The journey home felt like it was taking too long. Fynn was pushing to fly faster and fa'ster.

He landed in the Sagittarian quarter with a splash on the outskirts of the forest. He shifted into a giant cat and ran at the speed of light. Desperation had kicked in, he needed to warn the others. He needed to warn Kora. Ostara and Cedrick followed quickly beside him gushing through the wood like a white water rapid.

"Where is Kora?!" He yelled as he reached the gate. "I must speak to her now! Get everyone in the great hall!"

Ash rushed toward him "Kora is resting Fynn, I heard her in her chamber, she sounded ever so upset Fynn. I didn't want to disturb her." she said quietly.

"No, this is urgent, I must see her and everyone in the great hall," he repeated.

A loud bang at the door woke Kora again.

"Your Grace? It's Ash. You are needed in the great hall. Fynn has returned, he says it's urgent."

Kora quickly got out of bed and opened the door while straightening herself up.

"Did he say what's wrong Ash? Ash please, how many times? You do not need to call me anything other than my name. I am your friend." she said rushing down the grey stone hall, Ash struggling to keep up, plodding along behind her.

"No, he just seemed really worried and said it's urgent. That he needs to speak to everyone in the great hall."

The hall was already filled with soldiers and council members from each zodiac, Fynn waiting at the front with Cedrick and Ostara. Kora squeezed through the mass of bodies until she reached him. Feeling relieved that he had returned safely.

It fell silent in the room, and as Fynn explained the horrors he had seen. His voice seemed to echo and bounce from the stone pillars. Once he had finished everyone went into an uproar. Some were preaching bravery and how nothing will defeat them. Some were petrified and very vocal about it.

Kora stayed silent taking it all in and noticed the Virgo boy Art walking to the front to join Fynn.

He stood waiting for the room to grow silent again.

"Hush now everyone I believe Art here, has something to say!" Kora yelled as she looked around the room.

Art closed his eyes for a moment and everyone waited patiently. As he opened his eyes Kora could see a third eye glowing along with his others. His vision projecting into the air so that everyone can see what he sees.

"I am a seer, Virgo's can see what has been, what is, and what will come to pass," he said.

Everyone looked on in silence. Waiting for their future to be told.

"A lot of us will leave this place after a mighty battle with the Ophiuchus. But, there will be many sacrifices for this to happen."

Kora gazed at him, his hands clasped together, his nature so calm like a wise old elder.

He turned to Kora and explained the truth of what happens to the 'chosen ones', the betrothed. It was part of an annual ritual and feast. The Libran elders were unaware of the fact that the girls were being roasted and fed to the Ophiuchus royalty, lords and nobles. Part of the ritual was to strangle and choke the poor girls to death. Some were too impatient for the girl to be roasted and ate them alive.

Everyone remained silent, speechless. Kora turned on her heels and marched out of the hall and back to her chambers. She was furious. Pacing up and down. Frustrated that the elders had let this happen without questioning a thing. Just blindly doing as they were told.

She pulled her door open again. Kobi was standing to attention in the hallway.

"Kobi, head to the Libra forest, take a few men with you, bring the remaining Librans here. All of those that remain."

Kora demanded and watched him nod his head and stride off on his new mission, determination shining in his eyes.

CHAPTER SIXTEEN

From the Sagittarian Quarter to the Taurean Mountains the zodiacs had begun pitching tents, yurts and makeshift barracks to train for the impending war. Kora made sure they stayed clear from the lavender and violet fields so as not to damage them. The sweet smell scented the air for miles upon miles. The clinking and cracking of the wooden swords and spears created quite the noise whilst the soldiers were sparring against one another. The laughing, joking and chattering of the zodiacs made it feel almost like a festival and not preparations for battle.

The children of the zodiacs running, screaming and playing. There were some walking around with baskets of food sharing it out equally, others with barrels of water or ale for drinking, and the rest handing out clothing and weaponry being sure to reach every zodiac.

'This is what we need, friendship and balance,' she thought.

She had almost forgotten the great impending doom and sacrifice for just a moment. Trotting through on her horse with Ash and Fynn at her side acknowledging the occasional nods and smiles as she passed. Art had been staying in a yurt at the far end of the temporary settlement and had sent word asking to meet with her. She smiled and filled with pride as she saw her Libran dwellers waving among the masses.

She recalled Kobi telling her that it had been quite difficult persuading them all to come. They were too frightened at first, of being killed by the Ophiuchus.

The day star was beating down on them, it reminded her of their time in the desert, it made her feel thirsty. She had sent word for the Scorpio's and the Pisceans to join them again now. Everyone was coming together and she felt hopeful that she could save them.

Lifting the heavy cream sheet back to see Art sat in his yurt smiling gave her relief.

"You are smiling, Art? Does this mean that Goronn and his men were successful in saving the rest of your people?" Kora asked.

"It does your Grace, I have good news also. They will be returning along with the Gemini and Aries too in two days' time."

" Gemini? Aries?"

"Yes your grace, Goronn, and his men have freed the remaining zodiacs Gemini and Aries." He said as his eyes began to glow again.

"Oh, Kora! Goronn will be so pleased to have been a true warrior. I'm so proud of him!" squealed Ash with excitement.

"The Gemini are nimble warriors, childlike in appearance but stealthy and deadly. They have a special ability to multiply in two. They become twinned. This gives them a great advantage in battle and they can easily overwhelm the enemy. Aries are half ram, they are very strong and courageous like Tor." Art continued while showing Kora a vision of Goronn returning with them victoriously.

"Then we will be ready in four days as planned to march and finally face the Ophiuchus," Kora said firmly.

The time had finally come.

CHAPTER SEVENTEEN

Filled with determination, anger and fear Kora walks alone towards the entrance of Amoran city. Holding her hands up to show that she is unarmed, she steps cautiously barefooted on the cold stone pathway. Finding herself fixated on the path, slowly looking up she realises that she is surrounded by Ophiuchus guards.

"I am Kora, Prince Daimons betrothed. I have come to surrender".

She drops to her knees with her hands still in the air, ready to be shackled and escorted to a cell. The guards stand silent awaiting command as one slithers off to inform the Prince.

The guard returns and whispers to another that she is to be taken to the cells in the west wing. Both her arms are quickly in the grasp of a Serpent guard behind her back. The shackle pinches her skin on her wrist causing her to flinch. As she is being led through the grounds she glances around, scanning and observing the place. She is hopeful that she may see where Ailah and Nanuu are being held.

They enter the west wing cell block. The ground is ice cold and wet. It's dim, dark and dingy, she can barely see. Her eyes straining, she's looking through the iron bars of the cell doors and she catches a glimpse of Ailah, beaten, bruised and barely conscious. She gasps in horror as she's dragged in and thrown to the ground of her cell.

She sits waiting on the cold hard floor, her head bowed and hands clasped together as if she is praying. Lifting her head when she hears footsteps fast approaching her door. The door swings open and Prince Daimon enters. He charges towards her grabbing her by the throat and lifting her in the air. "You surrender do you? I was only just getting started with you". He throws her down like a rag doll and paces back and forth, deciding what to do with her. He looks at his guard and abruptly orders him to send a message for all zodiacs that they must come to Amoran city tomorrow at sundown to witness the death of their rebel Queen Kora. The guard nods and leaves sharply. Daimon stares at Kora for a moment in silence and without saying another word he leaves her curled in a ball on the floor.

As the door slams Kora lets out a muffled cry trying to hold back the tears and panic that is coursing through her body. She calms down and reminds herself that this is all part of her plan. Her troops are ready in place and waiting for the message.

That evening Kora hears a whisper coming through the wall from the next cell.
" Kora, my dear Kora. Is that you?"
"Ailah, are you ok? Is Nanuu Ok?"
Ailah responds " Yes we are in here together".
Kora cries "I am so happy you are alive, I have a plan to get us out".
"That's my courageous girl" a man's voice comments.
Kora is puzzled "who is that in there with you Ailah?".
"I am your father, Kora," he replies.

Ailah quickly says "Yes Kora, it is your father King Erald. We have much to discuss".

Kora reassures Ailah that she already knows the truth and understands. She continues speaking to Ailah, Nanuu and her father throughout the night informing them of the plan.

CHAPTER EIGHTEEN

The following morning the Ophiuchus guard informs King Erald that he will be executed alongside Kora at sundown. King Erald just stares at the guard and puts his head down. The day seems to drag but the sun begins to set. Kora and her father are dragged from their cells and taken to the main courtyard where the Ophiuchus King and Prince sit waiting to watch them die.

They are dragged up onto a platform, still shackled they are forced to their knees, side by side. All Kora can see is an ocean of eyes staring up at her, she spots Daimon straight ahead and glares at him, she then turns to her right to look at her father, she smiles and screams as loud as she can..."NOW!".

Zodiacs start jumping up from the crowd. First, the Cancerians charge into the crowd targeting the serpents, flinging all over the place. The Gemini begin dodging and weaving through slashing at the serpents with swords and daggers. Fynn appears from beneath the brawl and heads straight towards Kora and King Erald. The Aquarians quickly follow shifting into dozens of giant wild beasts quickly overwhelming the guards. Daimon jumps up in a panic, grabs his sword and ushers some serpents to come with him. He runs toward Kora fighting his way through the zodiacs. Fynn releases King Erald and Kora then hands her a weapon and says "let's get out of here".
"Not until we have Nanuu and Ailah".
King Erald says to Kora "go and free them I will hold the serpents off".

Kora and Fynn rush to set Nanuu and Ailah free, Kora requests Fynn take them to safety while she gets her father. Fynn agrees and shifts into a giant phoenix and takes off into the sky. Just as Kora returns to her father she sees him fighting with Daimon. Daimon quickly gets the better of him and stabs him through the gut. Kora screams in sorrow charging towards her father, she drops to her knees just as he lands on the ground taking his last breath he whispers to her "I am proud of you daughter, you can liberate the zodiacs".

Kora turns her head, spotting Daimon amongst the zodiacs who are still battling, lifts her weapon and runs at him screaming with rage. She swings her sword and slices his arm, he knocks her down, as he raises his sword to execute her, Ash him from behind throwing him into the soldiers he is knocked unconscious.

Ash lifts Kora and shouts "ZODIACS RETREAT… THE QUEEN IS SAVED".

CHAPTER NINETEEN

Weeks had passed, Kora stood and glanced from side to side at her friends. The army of zodiac soldiers behind them ready to go into battle and rebel against the serpents once more. Libran pennants snapping back and forth in the wind. This was the moment. This was the moment that justice would be served for her parents, for all the Libran's, and other creatures that were slain and tortured. It was time to finally defeat the Ophiuchus. She raised up the staff, holding it as high as she could. Standing glorious in her Libran armour.

"Charge!"

Her army began rushing forward to meet with the serpents. The staff lit up the sky and began raining lightning bolts down onto the Ophiuchus. Blowing them to smithereens.

The Sagittarians grouping together, filling the sky with arrows shooting through the enemy. Fire surging through the thousands of bodies before them. Aquarian's shifting together as one, in waves through the sea of soldiers drowning them as they went. Scorpio's roaring and raging through with their swords tearing them apart. Soldiers everywhere, blood streaming from their eyes and noses, pooling on the ground beneath them as they lay their eyes wide open and frozen in time. The smell filling the air, musky and rancid with death. Slavering salamander beasts dragging the carcasses along the ground, snapping their fangs and snarling.

"Roar!" Ash screamed. "Let's go!" as her and her kin charged forward swiping, hacking and slashing with their pincers.

Kora began to edge forward on her horse, winding the reins, tightly wrapping them around her fingers, the Serpent prince in her sights. She pointed her staff at him and yelled as loud as she could.

"Justice!"

The staff blew him off his mount and he rolled onto the floor. He quickly jumped to his feet and charged at Kora. She shot again with the staff.

"Ah!" She jumped down from her horse and yelled as he rose again, charged and jolted backward as they clashed. The prince just stared at her with shock in his eyes, she looked down to realise her staff had pierced right through his chest...

She looked back up quickly and suddenly heard a soldier screaming to retreat.

"Retreat! The Prince is hurt! Retreat!...Retreat!"

They swarmed around the prince and pulled him away from her staff. Rushing him off through the mud and slop on the floor. The battleground grew silent, a mist of blood still filling the air. All of the serpents scurried off running as fast as they could towards the city. She and her troops stood staring and watching as it dawned on them. They were victorious.

All her allies and friends began yelling and laughing whilst storming the settlement and releasing all of the Virgo prisoners. Roaring with happiness and relief. But, Kora remained silent. She knew that this wasn't over. That it was only the beginning.

CHAPTER TWENTY

Months had passed since the last battle with the Ophiuchus and Kora was growing impatient. Each week her army had grown from freeing the other zodiacs and so had she. She was no longer a young naive Libran forest dweller. She was now Queen of Hera. Luna had taught her everything she knew as well as her friends. Fynn and Ash shared the tales that they had heard growing up. But, Luna had actually lived it, so had dear old Cedrick and Tor. They had been living in the Sagittarian quarter waiting to take back the city. Growing the army and preparing all of the zodiacs.

"We must attack in a week's time. We have learned a lot about our enemy in recent months and received information that the Ophiuchus have their vessels docked around the city currently and we must commandeer them. It is time for the people of this planet to receive balance and justice in their lives. We will destroy the Ophiuchus and take the zodiacs to a new home." Kora demanded as she pushed the figurines of troops across the map. The commanders of her army all nodded in agreement.

"Fynn will lead the three thousand Aquarians and create a distraction in the centre of the city. Ash and the five thousand Cancerians will flank from the left and take out the tower. The Leo's and their commander Luca along with King Corin will flank from the right, we will use the phalanx formations with all of the dory's currently being fashioned for us," she continued.

Stopping for a moment to gaze around at everyone. She looked over at Fynn with such sincerity and thought to herself 'Not sure that I would have got this far without you my friend.'

"If you don't mind me saying now your grace, but this is our home now. We will be happy to go if you command but we would very much like to stay with you and I believe I speak for everyone in this room?" asked Luna as she peered around the room seeing the unanimous nods of agreement from everyone.

Kora recalled a dinner that she had recently had with Tor now that they were in better circumstances. He wasn't so angry and hateful anymore and had grown to love Kora. She had returned to the mountain with him to learn everything that he knew. As soon as he found out who she was, that she really was the daughter of his dear friend King Erald, he warmed to her even more. She had kept her history close to her heart when they had originally met properly. She didn't trust him. Tor told her of how the Ophiuchus and other zodiacs came to be on Hera. The Ophiuchus had sucked their own planet dry of all resources as Luna had told her before but she had now learned of the methods they used and what came after. They were a very intelligent civilisation and had created a technology that would pull energy from their own star which eventually killed their planet Laocoon. They set off to the stars in their vessels to find other planets to invade and settle on. Each planet and constellation they encountered, they eventually killed off and left. Taking prisoners and slaves from each, the zodiacs. Until they reached Hera. Kora was the only one that could save them now. Hera was dying, and the Ophiuchus was about to wipe out yet another planet and commandeering the vessels would be the only way to do so.

After explaining the devastating news to her allies. The deadline had been set for the troops to begin marching into their positions. The three thousand Saggitarians would divide up into centuries and help each phalanx. By shooting their ballistic arrows and normal arrows from the rear ranks.

"We must commandeer the vessels, as I said previously but we will need to work out a plan of action for these missions. They have a lot of vessels and an awful lot of soldiers to get past first. It feels like an almost impossible task. But, we must remain faithful that our endeavours will be successful."

CHAPTER TWENTY ONE

Four days had passed and the silent journey, filled with dread and worry had come to a close. The zodiacs would meet with the enemy on the battlefield again. The day star is at its highest. The deafening horns of war belted through the sky and bounced off the soldiers shields. Thousands of zodiacs stood in position awaiting Kora to give the command.

The horns stopped and the land grew silent. Kora began trotting up and down before the rows of zodiac soldiers.

"Today we take back control! she yelled

"No more will we be enslaved, oppressed and tortured for the Ophiuchus amusement! A new age is beginning! The age of the Zodiacs!" she cried out as she raised up her staff. It glowed and shot lightning down onto the serpents. Her soldiers were shouting and cheering. She circled around and pointed the staff toward the serpent army and the hoards began rushing forward.

Bodies flying everywhere, the ground grew soft and slippery, a stream of blood flowing in the trenches. Spears flying through the air in all directions. The phalanx of both armies colliding in a bloody mess. Heads being hacked off and rolling through the mud. The salamanders once again feasting on the carcasses and filling their bellies. Soldiers crawling through stabbing, hacking and slashing, faces splattered with blood and dirt. Once again the rancid smell of death filled the air, carried across by the wind.

At the foot of the vessels, the dead and injured bodies were stacked one on top of the other. Zodiacs scrambling over them as they would climb over the nearby hills and valleys. Not having time to stop and acknowledge or respect the dead. The serpents began rolling catapults forward shooting hellfire into the masses. The pain filled screams, cries, and groans floating across the land.

The zodiacs were outnumbered but not for long. Gemini began rushing forward, multiplying and swarming like ants. Using their twinning power to overwhelm the Ophiuchus and push them back and away from the first row of vessels.

Kora lunged forward giving the signal to the zodiacs to head for the vessels. Charging toward the foot of the vessel ahead of her, with Fynn and Ash by her side, fighting off the serpents and trampling any that stood in their way.

She whipped around with the staff, looking in all directions and she scrambled up the ramp, forcing open the stiff metal door. Turning back and glancing at her friends with a glisten of determination in her eye.
Ash stopped in her tracks, a look of shock spread across her face and she gasped as a spear pierced through her chest from back to front. Fynn dived toward the serpent behind her and thrust his sword quickly into his head.
Ash dropped to her knees after the devastating blow, looking down at her wound and then back at her friends. Kora let out a sorrow filled scream and ran back down the ramp and to her friend. Tears streaming, she grabbed Ash's face with both hands.

"You can't leave me, Ash! Get up and get on this vessel with us!" she cried.

Ash looked into Kora's eyes, no words came from her mouth. She released the remaining breath that she had. A look of peace on her face, and then she slumped over onto the ground. Fynn and a group of other zodiacs stopped and crowded around Ash's body slumped on the ground. They carefully lifted her into the air and slowly marched her onto the ship. Kora was on her knees screaming and wailing. Rocking back and forth hysterically unable to cope with this devastating blow. Soldiers dropping to the floor and bleeding out all around her. Tor ran through knocking the soldiers out of the way and scooped Kora up. He carried her onto the vessel and laid her down next to Ash. As Kora slumped over onto Ash she began to fill with an uncontrollable rage. She bolted upright and clambered to her feet, charged to the doorway and looked on at the scene before her. In the distance she could see King Corin of the Leo's fighting with the Prince. She grabbed a sword from the ground as she charged out and down the ramp. Running through the hoards with nothing but tunnel vision. She could only see him. Fynn and Tor ran beside her fighting off any serpent that had tried to swing for her. As she approached she lifted her sword and ran faster until...slam.

The Prince stares at Kora, his eyes locked onto hers. Blood trickled out of the side of his mouth, he let out a sigh and the life faded from him. Kora stumbled backward and as she did she ripped the ceremonial mace from his arm. Holding it up as high as she could she began to roar. King Corin, along with Fynn, Tor and all the Zodiacs joined her. Roaring for this small victory while the serpents retreated. Once Kora had let out her mighty roar she flopped into King Corin's arms. He looked down to see that she was wounded. The prince had stabbed her in the side as her blade met his heart. The King ran towards the vessel with her in his arms and she was laid next to Ash once again. Kora turned to look at her lifeless friend and let out the words 'I got him Ash' before blacking out...

"Come on now Kora, wake up! Ash would want us to be victorious, we have to press on. Her death will not be in vain," he said choking up and fighting back the tears.

Fynn held Kora tight and put his forehead on hers as if to pray silently. He got up and rushed to the control room of the vessel and quickly realised that he had no idea how to fly this ship. After randomly pressing at the buttons in a panic the engine began to hum and whirr. Fynn took the leaver, with a look of relief in his eyes and pulled it towards himself, he became unsteady on his feet as the ship jolted up into the air. The door to the vessel was still open, Art saw his chance to join them and grabbed the ladder as it lowered again.

"Now what do we do! "Fynn yelled as Art joined them.

"We fly up and destroy it!" Art yelled.
"Destroy what?!"

"The mechanism that is killing Hera and helping the serpents to dominate!"

Art scrambled to the seat beside Fynn.

"Up it is then," he said as he pulled the lever as far as he could and shot up into the sky.

The sky grew darker as they approached the atmosphere. Kora woke and rubbed her weary head and looked up and out of the window astounded at the size of the largest vessel above the city. A metal structure attached to it and connected to Hera's day star.

"They are draining the day star of its energy with that!"

Fynn got into position and began firing at the structure connecting the two until eventually, it blew, shattering into a thousand pieces that floated off into space. More vessels began lifting into the sky.

"The plan is working, the zodiacs are taking the vessels," Kora choked while holding her wound.
"We must fly back down and collect anyone missing." she continued as the other vessels began to fire unanimously at the mothership.

Fynn pushed the leaver and the vessel began to dive to the ground. He steadied it just in time and they floated along picking zodiacs up. The serpents had become severely overwhelmed by the Gemini and had retreated yet again. The vessel filled to capacity and Kora made sure the others did too. Finding a radio system that linked the ships, her and her people could now communicate. She sent a vessel to collect the elderly and the children from the camp.

Every zodiac still alive had now been freed from the serpent's grasp. The serpents had lost their control, their ships, their leaders and their mega structure that was draining the day star. They were now the prisoners on Hera.

CHAPTER TWENTY TWO

One hundred and sixty years we flew through space on the vessels searching for our new home, but really it was an instant flight in the grander scheme of things. We learned so much along the way, despite the journey passing us by very quickly, and we built strong friendships with our zodiac companions. We had learned that if the Virgo's stepped into the flight chamber in the control deck and projected the location that we intended to be, we would be transported there in an instant. Still, the time that we had spent gave us the opportunity to build communities within the vessels. The sights that we saw up there were awe-inspiring and I must say sometimes I miss it. I miss the adventure flying through the unknown and of finding our new home.

Commandeering the Ophiuchus vessels was supposed to be our ultimate victory. Gaining command of the ships gave us the opportunity to determine our future, to ensure the continued existence of all the zodiac races. It empowered us to seek a new and habitable dwelling away from Hera which the serpents had bled dry.

We happened upon Terra Mater, by accident really when studying the records. A perfect accident. The file fell onto the deck of the vessel and opened on the page. Terra Mater was a Roman goddess hence the name of this planet. It translates to Mother Earth. She looked beautiful in the files, even more so in person.

We lived in peace for six thousand years. Various zodiacs spread across the globe living among human tribes. There are many locations that we visit today that remind us of our dear friends and companions. You children of Earth, see them as mystical sights of lost and ancient super-civilizations. That's half correct I guess.

Sardinia, oh how I loved to visit Pearl and the Pisceans there. They built their beautiful city of Atlantis there before it dried up and was lost forever. The Sardinian people still have carnivals with tributes to the zodiac, to this day without even realizing it, the carnival of the Mamuthones. They worship Aries who also settled there.

Goronn and the Cancerians leaving their giant megaliths in Japan is one place that I like to visit. I believe a sword was found by the humans too, who think the sword was made for a giant. It belonged to Goronn himself.

The underground city in Turkey, that was home to the Aquarian's, it didn't take us long to build. Kora and the Libran's headed to the jungle and built the temples that the Mayans later moved into, she had found Nanuu and Ailah once we moved onto the vessel and was overjoyed to be reunited with them. The Saggitarians were roamers and loved to travel all over the planet, never staying in one place for long. The Cancerians also settled in Menorca, they built and lived in the Naveta d'es Tudons. Historians today believe that they are giant graves but, no they were once the homes and dwellings of the Cancerians. It was once a great megalithic city.
Norsun Tepe was built and inhabited by the Gemini, a glorious place to visit. The Leo's settled in Turkey in Alaca Hoyuk. The festivals and feasts were wonderful. But, sadly all of this has changed now.

After a year of being on Mother Earth, we traveled to the Dendera Temple in Egypt in order to officially crown our Queen at her royal zodiac coronation here on Earth. Art had seen the event in a vision and had advised that it should be held there. He did not see what was going to happen during the glorious event though. The zodiacs traveled from all corners of the globe to attend it and the pre celebrations and festivals lasted for weeks. As the day approached and we drew closer to the temple Art became overwhelmed with flashes and visions, as did the other Virgos.

He and the others knew that we needed to be there for the coronation and they were drawn to it for some unknown reason. Unknown until they walked into the temple to prepare the room so that it would be fit for the Queens Coronation. When we all walked in, all of the Virgos went into a trance-like state. Their third eyes projected to all of us as they stood around in a circle. The projection told us of a tale that the gods we had always believed in and worshipped were simply the caretakers of the constellations. Our original creator was Hathor. Once the tale had been told and the truth bared to us all the Virgos all dropped to the floor like exhausted animals. After some time of recovery, we continued with our celebrations and celebrated our newly found beliefs. We were supposed to be here. It wasn't an accident at all. The zodiacs were supposed to find Mother Earth and settle here. All that had happened to us was obviously a test. Others say that all that we had been through was to strengthen us and to prepare us for what lay ahead, even after all my years of life I do not know the answer to that. The coronation concluded and we returned to our new homes and continued to build and grow.

The Virgo's had decided to stay with Kora as her counsel and made sure that I would visit my dear friends often. During one of my stays with the Queen, Art had warned her of an impending attack. Their power gave us a great advantage to prepare but still, we did not account for the devastation that it would cause until it was too late.

Only a few of us original zodiacs remain now, and I felt that it was time to reveal to the human race, our children of Earth, how the zodiacs came about on this planet. It was us. We built this world.
Then it was taken from us again.

For four thousand years, we lived in peace and harmony. Kora's reign was just as it should have been on Hera. Everyone led balanced and wonderfully peaceful lives. She brought justice to those that needed it. She was a good ruler, a great Queen. Just as her parents had hoped, I believe.

The Ophiuchus found a way off of Hera and found us again and tried to take our beloved Mother Earth from us. We fought back with might and power and ultimately it destroyed the planet and brought on the great flood. Ninety-five percent of the population of all living creatures had died out. It was such a sad thing to witness. The Ophiuchus were defeated for good, but through all the devastation and extinction, Earth was saved.

117

Printed in Great Britain
by Amazon

82389593R00068